For Garden Seed
Stories and Reminiscences

For Garden Seed

Stories and Reminiscences

Janice Ruth Anchell

Cold Creek Press
U S A

Published by Cold Creek Press, Inc.
Monmouth, Ore.

For Garden Seed: Stories and Reminiscences

Library of Congress Control Number: 2022947938
Anchell, Janice R., author
Title: For Garden See: Stories and Reminiscences / Janice Ruth Anchell

ISBN: 978-0-9723443-4-0 (pbk)

1. Biography and Memoir 2. Short Stories 3. 1960s 4. Domestic 5. Family

Introduction by James Anchell
Edited by Steve Anchell and Kayla Anchell
Book design and cover by Steve Anchell

E-mail: info@coldcreekpress.com
www.coldcreekpress.com

Cold Creek Press

"All writing is autobiographical."
Henry Miller

Introduction

Sometime in the 1970s, during my teenage years, I stumbled upon a worn box hidden under a pile of old blankets in a windowless, dimly lit interior hallway linen closet. Curious, I kneeled on the carpeted floor, laying the box beside me. I felt a buzz of anticipation, for, at this age, many exciting secrets were still not yet revealed. Upon removing the top, I discovered that this forgotten treasure consisted of short stories that had been typed and stapled, and if the name appearing in the upper left-hand corner of each story could be believed, were written by ... my mother?

I read a paragraph or two of a randomly selected story and then another. Mom was a writer. Who knew?

Then, very carefully (I felt some guilt for snooping and worried about possible retribution), I returned the papers to their box and replaced the box under the stack of blankets exactly as it had been discovered. To my knowledge, the words in those stories remained stowed in that same box without being seen by another person for another fifty years.

I had little interest in my mom's writing because, at that age, the only thing that matters is oneself and one's own plans. I did have a conversation with Mom shortly afterward about my discovery, and though it was decades ago, I recall how she perked up and asked me eagerly, "Did you like them? Did you read the one about the woman buried at Forest Lawn? It's about a woman who's buried, and she's lonely because there's no one to talk to. I once heard someone say they wanted to be buried at Forest Lawn because they thought the view was beautiful. Don't you think that's funny?"

"Oh yeah, Mom. I bet it's great."

So, what's the story behind the woman who wrote the stories found in this book?

My mother, Janice Ruth Levick, was born May 12, 1927, in Vancouver, B.C. Her father, Julius Levick, a recently minted doctor from the University of Manitoba, was born in Russia in a city now known as Dnipro, located in central Ukraine. In Vancouver, he met his future wife, an accomplished violinist named Dena Weinberg.

Shortly afterward, Julius accepted a medical position in a small town in Oklahoma. Dena and Julius moved to Elk City where the first of their three children, Janice, was conceived.

Although she legally lived in the US, Dena felt anxiety about her lack of US citizenship and feared that she and her family might someday face deportation. If their child had been born in the states, the constitution would have guaranteed her automatic US citizenship. Dena and Julius, both Canadian citizens, could easily have applied for their daughter's dual citizenship. Dena must not have known this because, for reasons that remain unclear, she decided the best course of action to safeguard her family involved returning to Vancouver to give birth.

Consequently, Janice, who grew up in Oklahoma, spoke with a Southern accent, was a member of the Oklahoma

Rainbow Girls Society, and later became the band queen at the University of Oklahoma, had to return to Canada every two years to renew her visa to avoid deportation. She was what we today would call a "Dreamer."

Once, my mother confided to me that she felt sadness for her mother, as Dena was a gifted musician, who would have flourished in a big city like Vancouver, but instead was transplanted to a small town where her talent could not fully blossom. Nevertheless, Dena practiced her violin every morning for hours and found her creative, musical outlet by performing at local churches on Sundays. Dena passed away from cancer at the age of fifty. Heartsick, Julius followed a few years later.

Before passing, both Julius and Dena saw their eldest married. This came about in the 1940s, in the years after WWII, when another doctor from the East Coast, Melvin Anchell, answered the call for an opening at the same hospital in Elk City. Dr. Anchell was handsome, well-mannered, and Jewish. Therefore, it was not long after his arrival that he was invited to dinner at the home of Julius and Dena where, "entirely by coincidence," their stunning daughter, a radio journalism major at the University of Oklahoma, was home on break.

Melvin, an Army captain in World War II, was not known for indecision or half-hearted conviction, so within a month, he and Janice Ruth Levick eloped. As was the rule at that time, it was no longer sensible for women to finish college once they were married. Less frivolous and necessary work lay ahead of her–that of giving birth to children and keeping a home.

In the 1960s, Janice and Melvin decided to leave the South for California to escape the intolerable humidity and antisemitism. By now, their youngest (me) was a walking, talking, self-feeding human, so Janice had time to pursue her interest in writing.

Now in her mid-thirties, she enrolled in the writing class of a renowned playwright and writing instructor, Lajos Egri. Some of Egri's students—for example, Woody Allen—would later become famous for writing and other creative endeavors.

Lajos Egri passed in 1967 and so did Janice's short story writing career. For that reason, most of the stories found herein take place during the 1960s, in a place called Los Angeles, in a house on San Vicente Boulevard—a street that winds to the Pacific Ocean lined for miles with red-flowering coral trees.

It was more than five decades later, on my mother's 95th birthday, that she asked me to reach up into the closet of her home in Mission Viejo—many miles and many years from the house on San Vicente—to retrieve the same box that I had last seen in the darkened hallway.

Sitting on her couch together, she opened the box and searched for a particular story that she read aloud about a peach that she gave to me when I was a toddler. I felt a twinge of sadness, similar, I suppose, to the sadness my mother felt for Grandma Dena and her violin.

Before I left, I asked if I could take the stories back with me to my home in Portland, Oregon. I'm certain that even a few years earlier, she would not have allowed me to take this precious collection, which was so much a part of her.

But I think, sensing the long arc of her life, she wanted to pass something on by which to remember her. And that's how, working together with my brother Stephen and my daughter Kayla, this book came into being.

The creation of this book was a secret project to be presented to Mom on the Thanksgiving of her 95th year. Being a secret, we could not ask her to provide a title before publication.

There are two reasons for the title chosen, *For Garden Seed*. Primarily, it was an often used and comical exclamation of Mother's, who never uttered a vulgar word in her life. When exasperated, the worst expression she could muster was "For garden seed!" which is an acceptable replacement for the much more profane "For God's sake!"

The second reason is a tribute. A plant starts as an ambitious garden seed, initially focusing on its own growth and dreaming of becoming an expansive bush or towering tree. Frequently, the plant undergoes the costly process of flowering. The energy passed from the plant to grow the flower, which holds the seeds from which new plants will spring, depletes the plant of its own life force. The plant stops living entirely for itself and begins to live for the next generation.

Thank you, Mom, for giving us life and nurturing our growth.

And Mom, thanks for the peach.

James L. Anchell
Portland, Oregon
November 2022

Though, in many cases, the names have been changed, and artistic liberties were taken with the actual thoughts and words, my mother assures me that except for Ashes to Ashes, all the short stories in this anthology are based on actual events. ~JLA

Red to the Rind

"Lady, I done tol' you, ah cain't give you no watermelon less'n you has th' money."

My mother looked the driver straight in the eye and lied, "But, I live four flights up and I've left my purse. I'll pay you tomorrow."

"Ah'm sorry ma'am, but I got strict orders from th' boss man, cain't give no credit to no one."

I stood beside my mother in the dim Baltimore street while she argued with the negro. I knew even at the young age of six that there was no money up the four flights of stairs in the hot room we shared. It was Depression time, and there wasn't even money for the barest necessities. I had heard her plead for credit with the tradesmen in the block who sold milk and bread or with the current land-lord. It was unlike her to use her wiles for something like a watermelon, but both of us—lonely young woman and boy—needed that watermelon. There had to be something more for us than just existence, and at that moment, it rep-resented that something.

We stood at the window, Mom and me, trying to catch a breeze. It was mid-summer and in Baltimore, it can be stifling. We lived on the top floor above a cleaning shop and had no front steps, as our neighbors enjoyed. She had been gone all day, working in a factory. Every day she went there to work at a sewing machine from dawn till dark, leaving me with the lady next door. My father had died before I was born, and there were just the two of us. How I missed her when she left each morning, and I thought of nothing else during the day except her return. We meant a great deal to one another, for each was stronger and no longer alone when we were together.

Leaning across the windowsill, waiting for dusk, we heard, long before we saw him, the voice of the negro cry the familiar "*Watah* melon, red to th' rind. Get yo' *watah* melon." This was followed by the crisp clip-clop of hooves and around the corner came a straw-covered wagon pulled by a large, sweaty, white horse. The wheels of the wagon were upon the streetcar tracks, making it easier to pull. Piled high on the straw behind the driver were dark green watermelons from the Eastern Shore of Maryland. We watched the people leave their front steps and come into the street, magically pulled there by the cry of the negro and the promise of sweetness and cool refreshment.

The two of us were caught up in the excitement of the scene below us. We wanted without saying to become part of it, to have a watermelon of our own. My hand in hers, we ran down the four flights of darkened stairs.

My mother was pleading, "I promise to pay you tomorrow, I'll have the money when you come by."

"I'll sell you one tomorrow ma'am." His voice was even. You couldn't be sharp with a white woman, not in those days.

They were both lying, as the same watermelon vendor

seldom came by twice.

"I expect my husband home anytime and he'll pay you," she lied again.

"Ma'am, ah cain't wait, I got t'be movin' on. Please, ma'am, step back." He started up the wagon steps and the wagon began to move with his cry to giddyap.

"Please," my mother asked once more, "I swear I'll pay you tomorrow."

This was our method of survival, her pleading to her creditors, her entreaties to please trust her. More than once, it had kept us from going hungry. I had long ago accepted it as a way of life, not as a humiliation.

I don't know whether it was the sound of the streetcar bell in the distance that meant he would have to take his wagon off the tracks until it passed or the desperate look on my mother's face (or perhaps the wistfulness in mine), but he stopped and with a sigh asked, "Which one you all want?"

"You select it," my mother granted like a queen with her subject now that she was victorious.

He handed us one from under the seat of the wagon, apart from those on the straw. I remember thinking at the time that perhaps it was one he had set aside for himself. It was customary to have a watermelon plugged before its purchase, but under the circumstances, it was too much to ask. We carried our prize triumphantly to the hot little room on the top floor. There my mother cut it in half with our only knife.

Never before or since have I seen a watermelon like that

one. For when it was opened, we did not find the beautiful red velvety meat we so eagerly anticipated. Instead, it was an ugly gray color and filled with white worms. It had a putrefied, foul smell.

My mother wept that hot night in Baltimore, and so did I.

Locked Out

The window slammed down firmly in her face forcing her to jump back quickly in surprise. This was the first indication she had that she was locked out of the house, not by accident, but deliberately.

Pressing her face up against the glass Beth gently tapped against it and whispered, "Manny, Manny, please let me in."

There was no reply, but as her eyes began to focus on the darkened room, she could see him sitting stoically in his wheelchair, holding something in his hands.

"Manny," she said a little louder, "It's midnight, and I'm cold. Honey, please open the door."

She could see his face, lips pressed together grimly, eyes staring straight ahead, the knuckles of his hands white against the dark object he was holding. Once more, she walked around the house, checking the doors and windows, still finding none open.

Sick at heart, Beth sank down on a porch chair and pulled her coat closer against the night air. She was tired, it had been a hard day at the office, and now it was late. She wished she were asleep in her bed instead of playing some kind of game with Manny. The lights of the neighbors were on, but she didn't want the humiliation of trying to explain why she had been locked out, especially since she really didn't know herself. As for breaking a window, the thought of paying to have it replaced was unthinkable. It was all she could do to pay the rent and buy food and medicine since Manny had his accident.

What a way to end the day, first the trouble at the office and then Manny's objection to her monthly bowling session with the other secretaries in the office. It was her only night away each month, and she felt she had to have it if she were to maintain her sanity.

Manny, who had always been so virile and athletic, had refused to leave the house since he had become confined to a wheelchair. His only recreation was thumbing through old scrapbooks filled with pictures from his days on the high school football team or watching television. She knew how he felt; she really did. If only it were just his being crippled he had to overcome, but the Manny she had known—or thought she had known—when they first married was no more. Each passing day found him more embittered. He found ways to blame her for all his troubles.

Her neighbor's lights went out, and Beth, in a panic at being alone in the cold, dark night, once more pressed her face to the bedroom window and begged, "Please, Manny, you have no reason to do this, there weren't any men with our group. There never is. I've told you that." Then fearing her voice had carried in the night air, and she had been overheard, whispered, "If there's anything to explain, I will. Just let me in, please, honey."

She rapped on the glass, and this time it shattered under her clenched fist, cutting her hand. It wasn't a large cut, but tiny pieces of glass clung to her wrist, and she shuddered at the sudden pain.

She sat down on the steps, knees tucked under her chin, holding her injured hand. She had given Manny no reason to be jealous of her. One thing she would never be guilty of was being unfaithful to her husband. Her moral code just didn't allow it, no matter what the circumstances. Beth had always been outgoing but never could she bring herself to promiscuity. It was unthinkable. Knowing how possessive and insecure Manny was, she wouldn't even allow herself to have a cup of coffee with the opposite sex. It had been difficult when he was a whole man, but now it was impossible.

Each evening while she prepared dinner, the inquisition always began. He would wheel himself into the small kitchen and ask a perfectly ordinary question like, "Have a good day?"

Beth never gave him an answer without first weighing her words. It was like walking on eggshells; one wrong move and she was lost. "About the same, Manny," she would reply. Innocently, she might then say, "Marge had on a beautiful blue silk dress today."

Manny would counter with, "Guess that made you feel pretty bad since you can't afford a new pair of shoes, much less a dress."

"No, Manny, I didn't even think about it one way or another, just that it looked nice on her."

"Yeah, I guess I got something to be grateful for, can't have you looking too good, the men at the office would notice, and pretty soon that would be the end of us."

"Manny, I've told you, it isn't that kind of place, only a couple of men, and they're married. They just do their work and go home to their wives."

"I'll bet if there was someone available, you'd snatch him up pretty quick and get rid of me."

"Manny, I love you; why would I do such a thing?" She could feel hot tears behind her eyes at the hopelessness of the conversation.

"You don't love me; you're just staying with me out of pity or because no one else has come along yet. You can bet your bottom dollar you'll drop me like a hot potato if someone does."

There was no getting through to him; he was utterly miserable with himself and with her. She hadn't given up though; she felt like time, her love, and the right words would eventually make him see how wrong he was, but it surely wasn't easy. She had better give up the monthly bowling; she hadn't realized how much it disturbed him. The entire situation was absolutely ridiculous. He was the only thing that mattered in her life. Perhaps if it came from someone else, it would mean more to him.

She hadn't told Manny about the trouble at the office because she didn't want to worry him. This morning she had to fire one of the girls. It had been distasteful, but the girl simply couldn't do the work, and one of these days, she was bound to make a costly mistake. Beth dreaded firing her and had warned her more than once to be more careful with her work. Her name was Billie, but the other girls called her Bill because of her deep, masculine voice. There had been quite a scene when she had received her dismissal notice. Beth shuddered at the thought of it and was glad it was over. If she were going to be a supervisor, she would have to act like one, and firing people was part of the job.

Beth decided that since the glass was already broken, she would go ahead and break it some more. Gently, she broke off more pieces with the heel of her shoe. Reaching in, she unlocked and then raised the window. She could see Manny still sitting in the dark, watching her every move, glaring at her. His breathing sounded heavy in the quiet night. Just as she sat crouched in the window before jumping to the floor, she saw his hand raise, and in the moonlight, a glint of metal flashed in the room.

"Manny," she whispered, unbelieving, "what are you doing with that gun?"

For the first time he spoke, eyes narrowed and with hate in his voice that sent chills through her, "Get the hell out of here, you damn dirty tramp."

"Manny, for heaven's sake, what are you talking about?"

"You've lied to me for the last time. Your boyfriend, Bill called. Do you need to know more?"

Suddenly, the ludicrousness of the situation struck her. She, a grown woman, crouched in a window in the middle of the night, her husband pointing a gun at her, and all because he had mistaken the girl, Bill, at the office for a man. She must have called to see if Beth would take her back or give a reference. She began to laugh, but over the laughter she felt a hard punch in her stomach, followed by the sound of a gunshot. She felt herself fall and then heard another shot and saw Manny slump forward in his wheelchair.

"Poor, dear Manny," she thought before she lost consciousness, "I've simply got to make him understand tomorrow."

Lily White

Bert, the lifeguard, was admiring his reflection in the crazily angled mirror, meant to keep down any pilfering by the customers. He was leaning against the counter of one of the outdoor hamburger stands that dotted the beach, drinking his third Coke that morning. Over the rim of the paper cup, he surveyed what he thought of as his domain. It might as well be his, for he had been the summer lifeguard for this stretch of beach since he was nineteen and first started college.

He had just turned thirty and, for the first time, begun to assess himself seriously. It certainly made a difference to be thirty. No one had thought a thing of his being in school as long as he could still say he was in his twenties, but now his friends were chiding him and saying he was making a career of being a student. Originally, he had not intended to stay in school this long, but it had been so easy and pleasant living at home with his mom. Going to school in the winter, working here in the summer, taking only courses he liked, and not really caring about a degree one way or another had made the years glide by and kept any strain out of his life. All these things, plus the fact that the beach kids looked younger to him this summer than ever before, played a part in the reason why he had become so interested and curious about the girl who had started coming to the beach several weeks before.

He saw her now pulling into the parking lot and watched as she locked the door of her shiny red sports car. As she began walking toward the water, the thought crossed his mind that never had he seen anyone walk with such grace.

She was truly all woman and couldn't be compared to the young girls in their bikinis or even the ones at school in their dirty white sneakers. She was dressed like something out of a fashion magazine, wearing the sort of thing you might expect to find at the Riviera, and he wondered fleetingly why she chose this public beach instead of the private one down the road. An enigma not only because she failed to notice him as other women did, but not once had she removed her various long-sleeved silk shirts or slacks in the week she had been coming here. Each day she rented an umbrella from him, barely glancing his way when she paid the deposit. She sat under it for hours, alternately reading and watching the ocean. For someone to come out to the beach and not sun was bewildering to him.

To say he was fascinated would be putting it much too mildly. His waking moments were spent either looking at her or conjuring a way to get to know her. Sometimes she spoke briefly when renting the umbrella and her voice was low, melodious, and beautiful. Bert, or J. Roberts (as he had lately begun to think of himself), had never hesitated to pick up a girl that suited his fancy. To his consternation, he became an awkward, bashful, tongue-tied boy in her presence. This was confusing until he realized he had fallen crazily in love for the first time with a stranger who had done no more than rent an umbrella from him.

Like a prizefighter, he circled his quarry, waiting for an opening. That opening came a tortuous week later when she approached the umbrella stand, and he noticed the book under her arm to be one he had read in school. Gathering up all the love-sick courage within him, he announced he had read the very same book. After he set up her umbrella, he continued talking about the book, stammering a trifle in his attempt to appear suave and sophisticated.

Every day now, he sprawled at her feet like a puppy and talked about things in general. Soon she knew all about him, but all he knew about her was that her name was Lily. He never tired of looking at her long golden hair and deep blue eyes set in an alabaster complexion. What a combination they would make, he thought, he with his bronze tan and she so light. Lily, Fair Maid of Astolat, he called her to himself, and after she left each day, he would catch himself humming the old college song about the blue of her eyes and the gold of her hair. To J. Roberts, she had become the Mona Lisa, Venus, and the goddess of love, Aphrodite, all rolled into one.

He told his mother that he planned to get a steady job this fall instead of going back to school. He knew that whatever he wanted would be fine with her as long as he continued to live at home. As yet, he hadn't mentioned Lily. That would come later, and surely his mother would accept her when she realized what a good influence Lily had already been on him.

Arranging a meeting between the two women in his life posed a new and difficult problem. How could he ask a comparative stranger, especially someone fabulous like Lily, home to meet his mother? Surely, she would think he was mad even to make such a suggestion. But he wanted his relationship to go no further until he had his mother's approval.

He approached the subject casually because he did not want to appear too eager or too forward and because his ego could not stand a refusal. He chose his words carefully just in case she was reluctant he would lose face. She gave him no answer at first but instead looked squarely at him and then turned and stared silently out at the ocean. Thoughtfully, she reached for her beach bag, and from its depths, pulled out a small card case. She handed him a white, engraved card and smiled a crooked little half-smile while he read in disbelief.

THE PINK PANTHER A-GOGO
presents
MISS LILY WHITE
who bares all
(Nothing left to the imagination)
No minimum. No cover.

Lily finally spoke saying, "I have Monday night free; will that do?"

"Sure, sure," he gulped, backing away, the card still in his hand, "I'll be in touch, and we'll make it a date."

He turned away and fled from her view. Maybe he could get transferred to another part of the beach. Yes, that's what he'd do. A guy can't be too careful with that kind of girl around.

Ashes to Ashes

"How sweet it is," murmured Angie Potts, smiling to herself as she repeated a phrase of her favorite comedian. She snuggled down deeper in her pink, satin-lined coffin, six feet below the ground, collapsed her hands over her chest, and looked out at the scene below her. "Another funeral, how nice," she thought, "but drat, they're burying whomever it is across the way. At this rate, I'll never get anyone to talk to."

She hated to complain; after all, she was in Forest Lawn Cemetery, where she had always wanted to be buried. Angie loved people, all people, and people generally loved her. "When I die," she had often said, "I want my final resting place to be where there are lots of folks. Not only dead ones," she added, "but real live folks so I can keep in touch." For Angie's favorite pastime was people-watching. She could sit satisfied for hours on end in a hotel lobby, at a train or bus station, watching the people coming and going.

Sam, her husband, couldn't have picked a better place for her than Forest Lawn—what with all the movie stars buried there, the various museums, copies of famous statuaries, and above all, the souvenir shop. Why, the tourists just flocked there. She had heard it was rated second importance only to Disneyland. You could be proud of this place, all right. Never was there a dull day. The only thing missing was that Angie had no one to talk to. For some unknown reason, she was the lone person occupying this particular hill.

"Oh well," she comforted herself, "at the rate people are getting killed on the freeways, it won't be long until I'll have company."

The days without a single person to talk to stretched into weeks and from there to months. Always before, she had her husband or some friend to discuss what she had seen after a busy day of watching the world go by. She was dying to discuss the line of Rolls Royces that had just disappeared around the bend and to speculate with someone who the important personage in the hearse could be.

Just as she had begun to despair of ever having a companion, her prayers were answered. She had been dozing off one hot summer day when out of nowhere, she heard a thud on her coffin. There were two men digging a grave next to hers.

"Glory be, at last, someone will be here I can talk to."

The suspense was more than she could bear, and the next day dragged by slowly. That afternoon around 3:00, the funeral procession of her new neighbor arrived. She must be terribly important ... so many flowers, but she noticed an absence of tears among the newly departed friends and relatives. This latter information she filed away for later consideration.

"Ada Grubbs," she introduced herself as she was lowered into the freshly dug grave.

The reception she received from lonely Angie was over-whelming. She certainly was made to feel more than wel-come. They spent the first night and all the next day dis-cussing the various floral offerings placed on Ada's grave. The consensus of their opinions being that the dyed pink carnations were a trifle too gaudy, and the yellow mums had too much brown ribbon; but they did concede the pink roses were just right. Ada remarked that everything would have been much better had her cousin Sophie taken her advice and not used Glutts Florist. They always over-charged for what they gave you. She confided to Angie that Sophie never did anything right.

Two weeks later, Angie recalled the absence of tears at Ada's funeral and understood why this had been. Dear de-parted Ada had turned out to be what she and Sam always referred to as a professional nagger and complainer. Noth-ing whatsoever suited her. The hill was too sunny; why hadn't they planted more trees? Where were the caretakers when the children walked over their graves? She certainly saw no purpose in people reading all the names and dates and figuring out her age. This last complaint particularly annoyed Angie, who loved it when people would stop and read her name aloud, but good-natured soul that she was, she bit her tongue, counted to ten, and kept quiet.

One day in particular, the tirade from Ada Grubbs be-came especially bad and unbearable. She went on from dawn until dark, complaining about her coffin, the bad fit of her shroud, and just about anything that came to her mind. The old adage, "You can choose your friends but not your relatives," was certainly not true in this case. Poor Angie had become a captive friend and could do nothing about it.

How she longed to be alone again without the whining voice to interrupt her thoughts and to have once more the peaceful serenity she had felt before. She felt sorry for Ada Grubbs' husband, who had to put up with her all these years. She even speculated that perhaps he had something to do with Ada's untimely death, which had yet to be explained. Ada's gravestone showed her to be only fifty-five. Angie wouldn't have blamed him if, in a fit of rage, he had done away with her.

Early one morning, poor exasperated Angie was steeling herself for another day with venomous Angie when she heard once more the now familiar thud of a shovel digging.

"Hot dog," she thought, "we'll have someone else with us, and maybe this time it will be someone more satisfied."

But, to her amazement, they were digging up a screaming, maddened Ada. How dare they do this, she protested to unheeding ears.

"Why in the devil are we digging this one up?" inquired the first gravedigger.

"Because one of her relatives, a cousin or something, has accused her husband of poisoning her, and there's to be an autopsy."

So, she had guessed right; well, Ada certainly deserved whatever had occurred.

Since last month she's had two women, a man, and a child buried above and beside her—more folks than she ever dreamed of having, even in her wildest imagination. As for Ada Grubbs, someone else has been buried in her place. It seems her husband had her cremated after the autopsy when they didn't find any poison. She's now in a little bronze urn in the mausoleum.

Once more, it's peaceful on Angie Potts' hillside.

Rain, Rain Go Away

Rain, rain, go away because I'm burying my boy today.

Over and over, this stupid, childish refrain goes through my benumbed brain—haunting me, adding to my grief and guilt. Outside, the storm grows harder, the words change with the beat of the rain, and the chant becomes:

Rain, rain, go away, come again another day because I killed my boy today.

It seems as if it began a hundred years ago, but it was only last summer that Wilson's oldest boy, Tom, married Jane Bryan—a nice enough girl, who attended the local college, and whose only family was an aunt that lived on the other side of town. Our family had known the Wilsons for years. They were members of our church and had been friends of ours for longer than I can remember. The house next to ours was for sale, and we were pleased when the Wilsons bought it for Tom and his bride, and they became our new neighbors.

Jane quit school and kept house for Tom, who was working during the day and attending school at night. She wasn't much of a cook or housekeeper, and often she would ask my opinion about preparing food or advice on how to iron shirts. She was a small girl, barely five feet tall. She looked like a doll that might break if not treated gently. Everyone that met her felt immediately protective.

One evening on returning from a movie, my husband, Howard, and I heard music coming from the Wilson's house. As we pulled into our driveway, we could see a couple dancing through their lighted windows. I sighed and remarked on how romantic that was and added that Tom must have a free night from school. As the couple turned, I saw with horror that Jane Wilson wasn't dancing with Tom but with my seventeen-year-old son, Buddy.

"Howard!" I gasped, "Get Buddy home; what will the neighbors think?"

I watched as Howard knocked on the door, waited patiently for it to open, said a few words to someone, and then he and Buddy crossed the lawn to our house.

Screaming, I asked, "How could you mortify us like this?" and "Don't you realize that you're not supposed to be alone with a married woman when her husband's not at home?"

"Mother, you don't understand; she was lonely."

"Go to your room Buddy," Howard spoke grimly, "Don't ever let me find you in their house again when Tom isn't home."

This should have been the end of the incident. I discouraged her from coming over by being curt, cold, and always busy. Her visits became less and less frequent, and then she came not at all.

There was nothing I could do to stop Buddy from sitting on her front porch and talking to her in the afternoons when he came home from high school. Only if I interrupted him to perform some task or called him to dinner would he come home. Their laughter and low voices annoyed me. Twenty-year-old cradle snatcher, I thought. Why doesn't she just leave the boy alone?

At least six months had passed since the dancing incident when Buddy asked to speak with Howard and me about an important decision he had made. He told us the Wilsons were getting a divorce. So now I knew what he and Jane had been discussing so intently all week. He also informed us that he was in love with Jane and intended on marrying her if she would have him.

I wanted to scream and rage; demand he return to being the typical teenage boy he had been before that woman moved in next door. His studies, football, and the school prom were what he should be concerned about, not an about to be divorced woman. Instead, I spoke calmly and rationally, thinking to myself that once she moved away, she would be forgotten. My husband taking the cue from me also remained silent. There was no big fight but rather a drawing of the lines for the battle to come.

As I predicted, we heard nothing more about Jane Wilson after she moved. Buddy didn't speak of her, but he also didn't date any other girl.

Several weeks after his graduation from high school, he received a letter from her. My first impulse was to hide it, destroy it, but fearing I would be found out, I forcefully restrained myself and left it on his desk.

After dinner, he asked for another conference with Howard and me. The first real talk we'd had with him since he told us the Wilsons were to be divorced. He informed us that her letter said the divorce was official; Jane was back living with her aunt, and that he intended to date her.

"You'll do nothing of the kind!" Howard said. "Tom's father is a charter member of Rotary with me, and his mother has been in the garden club with your mother for years. The humiliation would be unbearable."

"Please try to understand," I said, "the Wilsons might even think you're the cause of the divorce."

"Mother, Dad," his voice was firm, "I'm going to see Jane no matter what anyone else thinks."

"I forbid you," these were strong words from me.

"It makes no difference. I love her. Nothing can keep us apart."

Dramatic words from a mere child, I thought. What does he know about love? He wouldn't know what to do if he had to support someone.

"You're going to have a difficult time, Son," Howard spoke, "because you won't be able to use our car."

"Then I'll walk."

This boy, who had to be reminded to mow the lawn or wash the car, found himself a job with a cleaning service to make money to take this girl out. Many times, I knew he walked late at night after the buses ceased to run, the ten miles back to our house after a date with her.

This madness will pass, we thought. He'll go away to college in the fall, and this nightmare will be over. Please let the summer go by fast, I prayed.

Tom Wilson saw Howard in the bank and barely acknowledged him. His father and mother were more direct; they spoke not at all. Our relations with Buddy deteriorated until we only nodded when he passed and mumbled at the table. We put every stumbling block in his way: no car, no money, and as a final blow, we had our telephone disconnected. Both Howard and I were hostile towards him and reminded him constantly of the difference in his and Jane's ages. It was no use; nothing deterred him. He still saw her almost every evening.

Things continued at an impasse until he was due to leave for school. Once more, he called a conference and spoke of his intentions of marrying Jane. They were both willing to wait until he finished college. Howard and I agreed this was fair and breathed a sigh of relief and hoped that he would meet another girl at school.

Buddy asked us for the forbidden car, and I realized this was the first favor he had asked of us. It was his last night home before he was to leave, and he wanted to do something special with Jane. I wavered and almost acquiesced, but a rule was a rule, and I wanted to continue showing my displeasure. I refused him the car. His father backed me up, and the decision was final.

It was 2 A.M. when the phone rang, and the ominous voice asked, "Is this the home of Buddy Lang?"

"Yes," I whispered, half asleep but desperately afraid.

"There's been an accident. Your son's been killed. Please come down to the station and identify him."

Yes, it was Buddy, my only child, in death as if asleep. They explained to us that he had been run over by a hit-and-run driver.

Oh my God, I cried, what have I done? I've killed my boy. Maybe if I'd been more understanding; if I hadn't cared so much what the Wilsons and the neighbors thought, maybe he would still be alive. Too late to think of that now.

What a dreadful day for a funeral. The rain is coming down in torrents. How can I put my beautiful boy in that cold, wet ground? And the childish phrase continues:

Rain, rain, go away, come again another day because I'm burying my boy today.

Free at Last

Pregnant with my fourth child, I rested in the window seat reading while the other three children took their afternoon naps. I was terrified, and with good reason. At a medical meeting the day before, I had heard Dr. Alton Ochsner from the well-known Ochsner Clinic in New Orleans tell hundreds of physicians and their wives of the perils of smoking. No fire and brimstone revivalist could have done it better. Dr. Ochsner's parting words to the group had been, "If you're foolish enough to continue smoking, be certain to get a chest x-ray every six months. If we find lung cancer early, there is a chance you might be saved by surgery."

Afterward, my husband, an M.D., had said, "What a shame, you're going to all the trouble of having these nice babies, and you may not be here to enjoy them when they are grown ... not the way you smoke."

It was true; I had to have my cigarettes. A perfect description of my habit was in the words Phil Harris sings, "Smoke, smoke, smoke that cigarette." The song continues, "Smoke yourself to death." I had started ten years before in high school. The sole reason for starting was that I thought it would make me more adult. On into college, I smoked, seeking out the professors that allowed you to "light up" during their lectures and who didn't mind teaching Milton and Keats in a choking atmosphere through a blue haze.

After my marriage, my husband, who was a non-smoker, made no secret of barely tolerating my smoking. Often, he would make remarks about its dangers, citing stories from medical school and how the students were able to tell which cadavers had been smokers. It seems the latter always had black lungs as opposed to the pink ones of non-smokers. This surely was a grim thought to contemplate.

Then would come the story all doctors tell about the fellow who contracted Buerger's Disease from smoking. The cure is to amputate the affected extremity. After losing first one arm and then the other, then his legs, and still refusing in spite of all this to give up smoking, the amputee finally becomes a basket case. He now sits outside the hospital each day and pleads, "Hey buddy, got a cigarette?"

Occasionally, I had tried to quit, and these efforts would last a few hours or even sometimes a couple of days, no longer. For I loved my cigarettes and had come to rely on them more and more. I couldn't have a thought, talk on the phone, or make a decision without my weed. I naively wondered how people could possibly drink a cup of coffee, have a cocktail, or play bridge without smoking. To me, they went hand-in-hand and couldn't be separated. Lately, my two little girls have been emulating me by putting cigarettes from the ashtray in their mouths and "acting like Mommy."

If I should accidentally find myself out of cigarettes, I would search through every purse and every pocket until I found one. No matter how old and hard, vile or stale tasting they were, I would be satisfied after they were lit. Failing to find one, I would go through the waste cans and ashtrays looking for a stub on which I would place a bobby pin or toothpick, and like Freddie the Freeloader have my smoke. I was addicted to tobacco as a dope addict is to heroin. The injury I was doing to myself just wasn't apparent.

As if it were fate, the magazine I was reading, sitting in the window seat that summer of 1954, was a recent issue of Reader's Digest, which had an article on the dangers of smoking. Everything combined, Dr. Ochsner's talk, my husband's foreboding words, the article I was reading, plus the fact that my mother had recently died from cancer, made me realize I was scared. Scared that I would get lung cancer from smoking and die a horrible death. The cigarette in my hand was only half-finished, but I reached for the ashtray and put it out. That was my last cigarette. Sound easy? It was the hardest thing I ever did.

I still had to face the beautiful people on TV commercials telling me each day what I was missing and how much more satisfying life would be if only I would try their brand of cigarette. At parties, theater intermissions, meetings of any kind, there was always the omnipresent smoker. At least if you decide to diet or give up alcohol, you can stay out of restaurants and bars. I know of no place where people don't eventually smoke. It wasn't willpower alone that abstained me from lighting up; it was my intellect that forced me to accept the truth. At least consciously, during my waking hours, I wasn't smoking. Nights were a different matter.

For at least four years following that summer, I dreamed night after night that I was smoking one cigarette after another and enjoying every single puff. Gradually my dreams changed, and I became so strong-willed in them that I could take one cigarette after dinner and be content. That one was all I needed. How proud I was of myself. Awake, I knew that if I ever did that "one," I would be lost, no different from an alcoholic and his one drink.

Finally, even that dream faded, and I haven't had it for years.

It has been eleven years since I stopped smoking, but I still love the smell of smoke. It took me longer to give up smoking in my unconscious mind than it did in my conscious self.

I don't believe I weigh any more than I would if I were smoking (A favorite argument of smokers, "I'd gain weight if I stopped."). I certainly can smell and taste much better, and my teeth and fingers are free from yellow nicotine stains. On a trip not so long ago, a friend who smokes asked to borrow my robe, and although she wore it only a few minutes, it reeked of tobacco when I put it on later. That's the way my clothes must have smelled for years; I just didn't have enough sense of smell to be aware of their condition.

I no longer feel deprived by not smoking. I can walk

miles without breathing hard, and even swim several lengths in a swimming pool. Best of all, I no longer have to fear an untimely death from lung cancer every day of my life. It's good to be free.

Pitfalls, Pains, and Pleasures of Publishing Your Own Book

My M.D. husband wrote a book entitled, How I Lost 36,000 Pounds which tells of his eighteen years' experience with overweight patients and the concepts he developed while helping them overcome this condition. We decided early this year that we would undertake the herculean task of publishing and distributing it ourselves.

The first thing we did was locate a printer recommended by a patient. After many long, tedious hours of talk he began to print our book, and we waited patiently to see our finished product. We pictured the printing, paper, and binding to be a cross between several fine books we had in our library. In fact, we had taken these same books to him, and he said that the finished product would not only be the same as these books but better.

Our very first setback came when the printer proudly showed us our book sans cover printed on paper, whose quality was only one step above newspaper. We couldn't believe our eyes. We rationalized that maybe it looks better slightly yellow; perhaps the paper being so thin is an advantage. After all, it's what's written in the book and not the way it looks that counts. All these excuses came from the fact that we had already paid the printer, plus we had deadlines to meet. Ads had to be prepared and placed. Our brother-in-law, who had business connections, had promised to place them in various stores if they were ready immediately. The final consensus was that it was too shoddy, and no self-respecting bookstore would accept it to sell.

We thumbed through a trade magazine for writers and found a printer two thousand miles away, but who had an honest-sounding ad. We called him, and he was sympathetic. Yes, he could produce, in shorter order—six weeks—the book just the way we thought it would be from the first printer. We drew up and signed an iron-clad contract on both sides, then sat back and chewed our nails for the next month and a half.

This was our first venture into the world of business, both of us having known nothing else but the white halls of the medical clinic my husband had owned and practiced in for eighteen years. If we had searched for years, I feel that we could not have found a more congenial business to learn in. Truly, bookstore owners are the ladies and gentlemen of the business world. Our new books were accepted with graciousness. They placed them on front shelves, on their counters, or in their window. When we took them streamers or posters to further our publicity, they placed them on their walls while we were still in the store and always with a smiling manner. What other business could you have attempted and been received in such a way?

Placing the books in the bookstore was but the beginning. We found they just sat without some kind of impetus. I sent the book to one of the leading columnists in our local newspaper. He wrote an entire column describing the book. This we received with mixed emotion. We needed to have the book mentioned, but he had lifted and printed the heart of the book, the diet, and this, my husband had found, was of no value without assimilating the rest of the contents of the book. There must have been many disappointed people who clipped the diet from the paper.

One of the things the column did do was reunite my husband with an old Army buddy, who read the article and called to ask was this the same Dr. Anchell who had been the regimental surgeon with the Seventh Cavalry in Tokyo? Yes, it most certainly was, and we arranged to get together. There was just one thing wrong; this old Army buddy was a very lovely woman who had been a colonel with the Red Cross in Japan during World War II. Can you even imagine your husband swapping war stories with a woman? On the plus side, she was with an advertising agency and offered to help us in every way she could.

Then while thumbing through my address book (looking for names of relatives I could write to tell about the book), I came upon a name I hadn't thought of in some time—the name of a girl with whom I had been corresponding for over twenty-five years, but had never met. We started as pen pals when we were twelve years old. I had found her name in the official Girl Scout magazine, asking someone to write to her. We had letters going back and forth through junior high, high school, and college. After we were married, we still wrote but having five children kept me too busy to write to people, much less someone I had never met in person.

I sent her a postcard describing the book, and she wrote back that she couldn't find it in the bookstores. This, by the way, is one whale of a problem doing the book by yourself because if you don't have any way to distribute your book, how can they be bought?

I sent her a copy of the book, and she replied that for the past five years, she had a radio and TV show of her own. Her viewers were constantly asking her how to lose weight and this book, *How I Lost 36,000 Pounds*, was the first book she had read that she felt she could recommend to her audience. She asked if we would send the book to the stores near her so they would be available to her listeners and viewers. Off they went from California to Massachusetts, and she has written that the first week she had over four hundred inquiries.

My husband has appeared on a radio show and was interviewed on TV for ten minutes, but recently came the big break. Pamela Mason's secretary called and asked if he would like to tape an hour show with her to discuss the book. When she called, Dr. Anchell was in the process of pumping poison out of a would-be suicide sixteen-year-old girl's stomach. While he pumped away, the nurse gave Pamela Mason's secretary the message that he would be delighted to appear with her.

Yesterday, the show was seen in Los Angeles. I suffered agonies throughout the entire hour. He said at one time on the show that people who are tense eat pleasure foods for tranquilizers. Do they! I was running into the kitchen during every commercial, looking for a cookie or a piece of cake. You would have thought it was me on the show. However, he did a masterful job and as one bookstore owner said when he called to reorder, "Whatever did you do? Leave the gate open? I've been flooded with calls for your book all morning."

Yes, we let the gates down and love it. The same show will be shown in New York City next month. How will we get distribution? We don't know yet, but we'll have it... I hope.

The Old War Buddy

What could possibly be better than having two old war buddies get together to spend an evening exchanging stories? Nothing, unless one of the "old" buddies happens to be a woman, and the other one your husband. Everyone else made men friends in the war, but not my Charles, his attachments were all apparently with the Red Cross volunteers.

She called at a most inopportune moment, as I had just put the baby in the tub. Forced to lift him out, and hold him towel-wrapped and wiggling (no easy feat) while she asked if the Charles Miller, who lived there was the same Mr. Miller who had been in Tokyo with the 7th Cavalry Regiment ... It was. She left her name and number and asked to have him call.

Charles had been in Tokyo several years before I met him, but I still felt pangs of regret that I hadn't been there to share Japan with him as we had shared everything else since our marriage.

Her name was Adele and when Charles returned her call they arranged to get together and talk over old times. Certainly, Charles informed me, I wouldn't mind if I didn't go along for their first get together, as I didn't know any of the people or places they had known, and I would surely be bored. I acquiesced, as I was sure this was Adele's idea, and I immediately took a great dislike to her.

The evening of their meeting was sheer torture for me. I asked myself why I was upset. What did I have to fear? It was just the idea of being excluded from anything Charles did. I was being left out. After I fed the children, put them to bed, and did the dishes, I tried to watch television. It was no use. I couldn't concentrate on anything. All I could do was look at the clock and wonder when he was coming home.

It had been the usual, long tedious day. The same rooms to clean, the same clothes to wash. After school, I had taxied the children to their music lessons, bought the same groceries, and it didn't help matters that the baby was teething, and a bottle of ink had spilled on the upstairs rug. I would have liked an evening out, too, and I resented being alone and longed for someone adult to talk with.

Charles came home a little after midnight. I managed a smile, although I was dying inside. We rarely stayed out after 10:30 because of the demands of Charles' office the next day. There wasn't much to tell me except that Adele hadn't changed noticeably in the fifteen years since they had covered the Tokyo countryside together in a jeep. We were invited to her apartment the coming Saturday for dinner, and I couldn't wait to meet this female who had found the fountain of youth.

Her apartment was nestled in the hills overlooking the fairyland that is Los Angeles at night. Everything was luxurious, selected with great taste, and I thought, "Why not? She has no children to ruin it."

A divorcee, she was a tall, statuesque brunette, who could have stepped from the cover of *Vogue* magazine. Glamorous to her toes, she was a sight to behold.

She greeted me with: "I just simply couldn't believe dear Charles was married; he just didn't seem the type to ever settle down. and to have three children. Unbelievable!" She said it as if only peasants had three children.

She was everything I wasn't but longed to be. My dress that always made me feel chic, now resembled a bathrobe. Even her world was exciting. She was in advertising; she met exciting people every day of her life—people who traveled, who were creative, who were interesting to be around.

The food she served was exotic, as I knew it would be, and served beautifully by her live-in maid. There was nothing, whatsoever, to mar the perfection of the household. Charles, sitting before the open fire after dinner, sipping brandy, looked as if he belonged here. I was frightened because for a minute I couldn't picture him in the role of father and husband, where I had placed him. He couldn't help but wonder why I couldn't look like Adele and do things the way she did. I could not help but wonder if he was regretting our marriage.

The conversation was brilliant and witty. I, who barely had time to glance at the headlines of the newspaper, could add nothing to it. All of a sudden, I hated myself, my life, the eternal cleaning and cooking. Most of all, I resented being taken for granted by my children and husband.

After we left, I talked with Charles about my dissatisfaction, but he soothed and placated me with all the old cliches: the grass looks greener on the other side; all that glitters is not gold. He reminded me that having a husband and children was far more fulfilling to a woman than a handful of friends and a maid. Then he said he loved me, which made me content with my lot in life—that of wife and mother.

Since our visit to Adele's, we've moved to a house in the hills that has a view. I've bought a lot of new clothes, and really look spectacular in my hostess pajamas, especially when I'm using my cigarette holder. I don't taxi the children anymore; they can walk if they have to go anywhere. I've been watching the ads in the paper, and as soon as something in an advertising firm comes up, I'll apply. Not that I'm serious about working, I'd answer the ad just for fun.

Second Chance

Old Charlie Fischer shivered in the winter sun as he sat on a bench fronting the Pacific Ocean. Once more, he read the letter that had caused him so much anguish. It had come three months ago, delivered by a new postman. A portent of things to come, Old Charlie had thought later.

The envelope, large, stamped with the seal of the city, frightened Charlie, who was unused to receiving mail of any kind with the exception of his monthly pension check. Everyone he had ever cared about, or who had ever cared for him, had passed away one by one, long ago.

Unbelieving, Charlie's faded blue eyes read that his apartment building was scheduled to be torn down. Further on, it told him he had ninety days in which to find a new place to live.

"Progress comes to Venice!" screamed the evening paper vendors. The morning papers caustically echoed their sister publication by headlining "Slum Clearance to Make Way for High Rise Apartments." Everyone seemed to be very happy about the entire situation except Charlie and his friends who occupied these so-called slums.

Twenty-some years ago, when his wife Martha had died, he had closed down his shoe repair shop in Illinois and had come to spend the rest of his life in California. His home now was one of many old red brick apartments looking out over the ocean. It was his practice, as well as hundreds of other tenants, to sit each day for hours in the sun on the benches that lined the boardwalk. They never tired of watching the ocean, finding peace and security in its constancy. There were never-ending checker and chess games; you could always find someone ready to play.

No one worked. They were all pensioners like himself, retired from the busy world that they hardly knew existed outside of their daily newspapers. The long, lovely days were spent with great satisfaction. It was pleasure enough just to be with one's companions among the beauty of the cliffs that curved from the shoreline.

For a few days, everyone was stunned. Where would they go? What indeed could they find for their meager pension money that would equal what they had found in Venice by the seashore? Were they destined now to the slums of Los Angeles or to the back rooms of their various relatives? Here they were free from dependence on others.

Surely, they argued, a city this big with so many miles of coastline could get along without this tiny sacred stretch of land. Never once had they thought of themselves as being slum dwellers. It mattered not to them if the buildings were old and ramshackle, the beds cheap iron, the curtains old and frayed. For outside their rooms was a beautiful world, filled with graceful seagulls, blue ocean, and white, clean sand. Their meager pensions would never allow them to find such a utopia again. Protesting their plight would be valueless. They knew their feelings were of little significance to the city fathers and of influence they had none.

One by one, Charlie Fischer's friends left the old apartment houses. Each one going to a different and distant place. The days became lonelier and lonelier as the familiar faces failed to appear. Finally, there was no one left but Old Charlie and Beau Smith, who had a daughter coming after him in the morning. There they sat until late into the cool night. They talked of old times, of the checker games Charlie loved so well, of everything except the future. When they parted, they promised to keep in touch, although both knew that this was the last time they would be together.

Early the next morning, the wrecking crews came with their bulldozers and other equipment. The despair Charlie felt knew no bounds. Each pound of the cement ball was like a thud against his heart. Each wall that crumbled brought an agonizing ache to the pit of his stomach.

Charlie, who had always been patient and gentle, could stand no more. He cried out against these men who threatened his existence. He rushed forward, wanting to hurt them as they were hurting him. Suddenly, he felt old and tired and helpless and embarrassed. Turning, he fled the scene of devastation. Tears fell softly on his cheeks and then damply onto his sweater.

Old Charlie had absolutely refused to admit any thought of the future or to accept that he must leave his beloved beach. Starting over again at his age had been too painful to face. He had no plan.

"I'll go by Chan's Grocery and talk with him," he thought. "It will help to be comforted, and maybe he can tell me what to do."

Chan, a longtime acquaintance, wasn't much consolation. His small grocery was also to fall under the wheels of progress. Even now, he was busy preparing to leave and join his brother in a store on the other side of Los Angeles. He did, however, offer Charlie temporary shelter in the back of his store.

After dinner, Charlie returned to the beach, where only early this morning, his familiar apartment had stood. In the moonlit night stood a heap of rubble, the only remains of the home he had known for so long. All were gone—the friends, the good times, the blessed apartment.

Charlie looked once more at the cliffs, the palm trees etched against the night sky. The loneliness he felt at this moment was terrifying and unbearable.

Reason left him, and he walked slowly toward the dark ocean. The water was cold. Strange, he hadn't expected it to be so cold. For although it was as familiar as his old worn sweater, he seldom went in. He felt no regret but instead welcomed his decision. Better to die this way, he thought, rather than spend his few remaining years in an unknown place, far away, among strangers. The ocean was the only friend he had left. At last, he was beginning to feel warmer.

"Ah, sweet, blessed ocean," he mused, "hold me to your bosom, rock me, as my mother used to do." The sea was lapping about his head; the water stung his eyes.

Suddenly, the calm was broken by hoarse screams in the dark, "For God's sake, help us!" Charlie's eyes, now used to the dark, made out the shadowy figure of a boat adrift in the water. "Help, we're sinking. Please, someone help!"

Shocked from his reverie with death, all thoughts of dying gone, he waded back to shore. His clothes were cold and clinging to his body as he raced down the beach to the nearest telephone to alert the Coast Guard. Thank heavens, he sighed.

Old Charlie, his stark white hair plastered against his face, stood shivering in the night until help appeared, and he was able to point out the place where he had seen the boat. In a matter of minutes, a rescue had been accomplished. The rescued were a man, his wife, and their two young sons. It seemed their houseboat had lost its steering power, and they had been drifting aimlessly. All were thoroughly frightened.

"Damn boat, damn boat," the man muttered as he comforted his wife and children.

As he left the beach with his family, he turned back to thank Charlie, who stood shaking under a blanket. At the same time, one of the Coast Guard hollered that the boat was saved; what should they do with it?

"You want it?" he asked Charlie. Charlie nodded, his teeth chattering. "Take it; she's been nothing but trouble since the day I got her. The papers are in the cabin." With that, the four of them left the beach without a backward glance.

Should you happen to be down in Venice anytime soon, be sure to look up Old Charlie Fischer. He shouldn't be hard to find. Charlie and his houseboat "Second Chance"

have almost become a landmark there. Strangers often remark at the incongruity of a houseboat beached among all
the glittering glass and steel girders of the new high-rise
apartments. This doesn't bother Charlie. He knows he belongs there and plans to stay.

Doug, Fourth Child, Second Son

When he came home with a bad report card, my husband and I declared that Doug could not have a birthday party, not until his grades were brought up. Unthinking, we had selected the worst punishment possible to mete out to Douglas, who would be ten the next week.

In every large family, without fail, is a child with no special position such as the eldest or youngest enjoys. In our family of five children, his name is Douglas, the second of three boys. Lacking status, through no fault of his own, special occasions such as his birthday have extra meaning since it's his day and his day alone.

We think of him as our good boy because he gets along well with everyone in the family and his friends at school. There is always someone knocking at the door asking if he can come out to play. He's in great demand because of his even temper and pleasant ways. A bit of a Beau Brummel, he loves to be dressed properly and takes great pride in new clothes. He collects coins, and it can be maddening watching him examine each penny before it is spent to make certain none of us is throwing away a coin of great value.

His one claim to fame is the French horn he plays in the school orchestra. Any attention given to him is soaked up like a sponge. Sometimes, because Douglas is so loving and undemanding, he gets lost in the shuffle and gets taken for granted.

As his day approached, a very real pall fell over the house, the children tiptoeing and whispering and then asking couldn't we please relent and let Doug have his party.? No, we couldn't change the punishment; Douglas would have to learn more responsibility at school. It's difficult to back down after taking such a definite stand; harder to be a proper parent.

His birthday dawned as any other day; no special plans were made. After dinner, his father presented him with a small camera and managed to receive a polite thank you from Doug, who afterward went promptly up to his room to study. We all felt pangs of remorse because, for weeks, he had been talking about whom he was going to invite and precisely what games were to be played, the kind of favors, and what was to be served. Months before, he had started asking me daily how many days until his birthday.

After dinner, our eldest daughter suggested that her daddy and I drive to the beach as we often do in the evening. When we left, it was like leaving a house with a death in the family, not a smile or goodbye from anyone.

An hour or so later, we returned. As expected, all the lights were off. I went upstairs to say goodnight to the children. The boys' room was empty, but there was a light under the girls' door. Opening the door, I saw the loveliest, most heart-warming sight I had ever witnessed. The other children had decorated the bedroom with colored streamers and balloons hanging from the ceiling. A beautiful, day-old bakery cake, purchased with their precious savings, was being served not only to my five but to the two maids that worked at houses on either side of ours. They had been invited to swell the guest list. In the midst of this was bright-eyed, beaming Douglas, presents piled high, all treasured possessions belonging to his brothers and sisters, wrapped up and given to him for this special occasion.

What can you say or do when something so lovely happens that gives proof of the closeness and beauty of having a family? That makes everything worthwhile. These five, so often at odds, closing ranks was truly amazing. So totally unexpected … or was it?

Garbage
(The Terror and Euphoria
of a Housewife)

My contention has always been that an empty garbage can is a thing of beauty. I can't help admiring one that stands militarily beside its brethren, lid on straight, waiting patiently for someone to fill it. The first of each week, they appear bottomless, but always in a matter of days, it's necessary for me to scrounge around to find room in one.

It's a matter of record, and to my chagrin that no matter how many garbage cans I buy, I never have enough. When it's time for the garbage truck to make its weekly rounds, mine are always overflowing. Seldom is there one inch of extra space where I can empty all the waste cans still in the house.

Where to put the blame for this household dilemma has always been a serious problem for me. There was a time that I thought it might be due to the two newspapers we receive daily. For one month, I carefully folded each and every one of them, tied them neatly with string, and placed them beside the garbage cans. This made absolutely no difference; the cans were as full as before. Then I placed the blame on the gardener, who put all the grass clippings in the cans. Ever since he carts away what he cuts with a now-you'll-see attitude, and still the cans are full.

If there is no place to put them, what do you do with yesterday's crumpled newspapers, empty pickle jars, bread wrappers, and empty shoeboxes? They can't be piled in a corner and forgotten. I've found myself wandering from room to room, hands full of garbage, looking for some kind of receptacle. Nothing is solved when finally, in quiet desperation, you set everything down outdoors beside the already overflowing garbage cans, knowing full well that no self-respecting garbage man will take them loose like that. The only grace is that at least it's out of the house.

The excess could be placed in corrugated cardboard boxes. But somehow, the boxes I bring from the grocery store for this purpose have been found long ago and cut up by my children to make trains or forts. Why not go ahead and buy an extra garbage can every time I need one? Only because I can foresee disaster in such an indulgence. It is conceivable that in no time, I would have my driveway filled with garbage cans and with no room for the car. Besides, it's necessary to carry each and every one to the curb the day the trash is collected and carry them back when they are emptied. It is not without reason to surmise that in no time at all, I would have as many as twenty-five or more garbage cans, all full.

Breathes there a housewife so tranquil that she has not been heartsick and struck with dismay when she hears the garbage truck go by and realizes she has forgotten to put the cans out the night before? For me, nothing can be more catastrophic.

On occasion, I have had to put the cans in the back seat

of my car and drive up and down the streets until I find the garbage truck. You cannot conceive the odor of driving in a car filled with garbage. Sometimes I don't find the truck on my street but must follow it into another neighborhood. The people who don't know me come out of their houses to see the stranger take garbage cans from her car. I try to appear nonchalant about the entire situation. They probably think I live in my car and have no place for my trash to be picked up, so simply dump it in the most convenient truck I can find passing by.

Next in disaster, but equal importance as missing the truck, is having your cans filled two days before the pickup is due. A trick of the trade is to make friends with someone who gets his garbage picked up on another day than you do. That way, you can always take your cans over to her house to have them emptied by her trash man.

Other disasters listed in order of importance are: one, your garbage day falls on a holiday, and your garbage isn't picked up until the next time around; two, it rains, and whoever was the last one to take out the garbage forgot to put the lids back on; three, your neighbor's dog gets loose and turns over your garbage cans.

I lived once in a neighborhood where most of the couples worked. Consequently, they would leave home early in the morning and forget to put out their garbage cans. Each spouse would blame the other for this oversight, which I felt led to at least one divorce. Realizing the seriousness of this neglect and in the interests of family harmony, I became a one-person vigilante. Like Paul Revere,

I would stand outside on the block on that important day of days crying, "The garbage man is coming." To which all would respond by dashing to the curb in all manners of dress, dragging their cans behind them. When I moved away, I wondered what would become of their garbage without someone to remind them.

Sometimes I drive by houses that have one or two tiny trash cans at their curb, so small that five of them would fit into one of mine. What kind of people are these with so little rubbish? Do they not eat nor read as I do? Are the clothes they purchase carried home without wrappings? Who could live for one week so meagerly and have but one-half gallon of garbage? Is it too far-fetched to suppose that they are putting their excess in my cans in the dead of night? Either that or their lives must be so sterile that rather than envy them their garbageless existence, I should rejoice that my life, unlike theirs, is full. Full, I might add, of filled garbage cans.

The Dream

Max Abrams, the cantor of Temple Beth Hillel, was awakened by a frightful nightmare. It seemed so real that even when he was fully awake, his mouth felt dry, and his heart continued to pound furiously against his chest. In the nightmare, he saw himself standing in the pulpit singing the beautiful psalms of Rosh Hashanah. His voice had been perfect, the tones pear-shaped, so poignant and sad they brought tears to the eyes of every listener. When it came time for him to blow the shofar, he found that no matter how hard he tried, no sound would come out. He blew until his lungs ached, and his face was red. Looking out into the congregation, hoping to find understanding and sympathy from the people he knew so well, he saw instead strangers whispering together and heard embarrassed, polite laughter and derisive snickers.

It was then he woke up.

The cantor was quite relieved to find it was only a dream, but he found it difficult to forget. Only the day before, the rabbi had called him into his study and introduced him to Mr. Davidson, who came from a large city.

Mr. Davidson had said, "Your reputation as a cantor has followed you, Mr. Abrams, and that is exactly why I am here."

The cantor replied, "Thank you, I am flattered that I am

known; this is such a small, out-of-the-way place."

"I came to invite you," Mr. Davidson continued, "to sing the Rosh Hashanah services and to blow the shofar at my temple to announce the new year. A delegation has been selected to judge you, and if all goes well, we would like you to come to our city permanently and be the cantor of our synagogue."

"Mr. Davidson, I am pleased that you want me, but I am needed here. If I should leave the temple, the people here would have no cantor for high holidays."

The rabbi replied, "No, Max, this is a great opportunity for you, and if you are accepted, great fame would come to you and honor to this temple."

Instead of rejoicing, Cantor Abrams felt sad at the news that he might soon be leaving. He loved the small city and the congregation that he served, but he was determined to do whatever was best for the temple; if it was bringing them honor, then that was what he would do.

That night the cantor's nightmare returned. This time as he looked down into the unfamiliar congregation, he saw the delegation from the far-off city. Set apart by their black suits, they were seated in the front row. They were nodding in pleasure as his voice sang the beautiful service, but once again, when he blew the shofar, no sound came out. It was unthinkable that he could not blow the shofar. He saw the delegation stiffen and could hear them click their tongues on the roof of their mouths. With this, he woke up.

Blowing the shofar was not only a Hebrew tradition but one handed down in his family. His father and grandfather before him had always blown it on the high holidays. They had both been big men able to make the earth tremble when they blew the ram's horn. There was never any doubt left in anyone's mind that the Day of Atonement was there. Cantor Abrams hadn't inherited their stature, he was small in frame, but from them, he learned the art of blowing the shofar. He was the first man in his family to become a cantor. When he blew the shofar, and the notes came out loud and clear, he felt as tall as any man.

On awakening from this last nightmare, he found himself covered in cold sweat. He was frightened at the humiliation he had suffered at the hand of the dream congregation. Dressing quickly, he went back to the temple. Taking the shofar down from its case, he tried to blow it. Always before, it had responded to his lips, but nothing happened now. I must be out of practice, he thought, and the dream was a warning to me. Try as he might, he was only able to produce small, muffled, squeaky sounds. Whatever could have happened, he asked himself. He sang a few notes. His singing voice was as beautiful as ever. He was proud of the fact that when he sang Kol Nidre on Yom Kippur night, there was never a dry eye in the house. Now the ram's horn, which must be blown not once, but many times during the service, refused to respond. Cantor Abrams went home a very troubled man.

Once more, he dreamed, only this time the delegation in its dark suits stood as a man and walked out. The entire congregation whispered, "Shame, shame."

In the morning, he went to the rabbi and asked for

permission to go into the country for a few days. It was agreed he should go and come back rested. His acceptance by the temple in the big city would mean a great deal to him. The man selected to be their cantor could not help but gain fame.

That night the cantor packed his clothes, took the family shofar, and went off into the countryside. He secured a room at a farmhouse, and that night at his host's request he sang lovely old Hebrew songs for the family. The pleasant evening was marred, however, because after he went to bed his nightmare recurred. This time, after failing to blow the shofar, not only did the delegation walk out, but the president of the temple who was seated on the podium stepped forward and removed the cantor's white tallis from his shoulders and his yarmulke from his head. The shame he felt was unbearable.

The next morning, a very despondent cantor took the shofar and walked far into the woods. He was seated with his back against a tree contemplating. Coming through the woods he saw his host's small son appear, who as he approached asked him, "What are you going to do? Blow the shofar? All our family, and all our neighbors are coming into town for the holidays, we will be there to hear you sing."

They would be there, but he wouldn't. The cantor couldn't bring himself to tell the boy that he wouldn't be at the temple to usher in the new year.

Suddenly, he realized that he didn't want to leave the familiarity of the small temple and exchange it for the fame of the larger place. He sighed a sigh of relief and for the first time in days felt relaxed. Placing the shofar to his lips, he brought forth pure magical sounds from the horn. He realized that his nightmares had not been caused by the eating of gefilte fish or too much kugel before bedtime, as he had half-way suspected, but from his fear of leaving good friends. Hurriedly, he returned to town to tell the rabbi of his decision.

That Rosh Hashanah day the rabbi told the congregation that every man must serve a cause for an ideal that will outlive him. He went on to say, "We are surrounded by a terrifying sea of chaos, and only by rendering deeds of service in our private worlds can we beat off the sense of loneliness and terror from our hearts."

It must be said here that on Rosh Hashanah morning, not only was the congregation from Beth Hillel favored with the cantor's magnificent voice, but many were overheard to remark that never had they heard the shofar sound more clearly or sweetly.

Stolen Hours

"Mother, I don't suppose you could drive Kelvin and me to the model airplane flying field, tomorrow?" A simple request from Stephen, my fourteen-year-old son, but asked hesitatingly.

Time is a precious commodity that I never seem to have enough of, and perhaps because I was feeling guilty, I sent the control tower of my mind into motion, clearing away all the many things I always have to do. In a matter of seconds, I realized that number one, tomorrow was Sunday and that if number two, I put on a roast instead of stuffing a turkey, I would be free for half an hour anyway. At least I thought it would be a half-hour; I couldn't have been more mistaken.

Stephen's interest in model planes didn't surprise me; he had been putting them together since he was five. However, lately, instead of the plastic models which did nothing more than adorn a shelf, he had been tediously putting together a large plane made of balsa wood and tissue paper.

The next morning, after picking up Kelvin, his compadre in all things, I asked which way I was to go.

"Straight out the freeway," they replied, pointing toward the valley.

It wasn't until I had gone over ten miles that I realized I had made the mistake of not asking just how far this field was anyway. A few miles more and we turned off the freeway, soon leaving the Sunday traffic behind. A turn to the left off the paved road onto a dirt road, several more miles across an open field, driving carefully because of the delicate planes we carried. Suddenly, we went over a rise, curved slightly, and there before us was an entirely different world from the one we had just left.

There were hundreds of cars parked every which way, with double that many fathers and sons whose mothers and sisters were enchantedly watching the flights of their planes. Five landing fields were spread far apart, each one made of concrete, much like their real counterparts. Each one was designed specifically for different types of planes. Around each strip, the spectators sat in lawn chairs, brought from their backyards, already eating lunch from the boxes by their sides.

The largest landing field was by far the most exciting. Planes whose wing spreads measured three to six feet across were taking off and landing much as they would at an airport. Radio-controlled, they were diving and looping, spinning and flipping—their bright red and yellow, orange and black wings silhouetted against the deep blue sky.

Fascinated, I forgot the roast getting overdone in the oven, the minutes I had to type for a meeting the next day, and the closet that needed straightening. Instead, when Stephen asked that I come back for them in two hours, I told him that I would wait. I sat on the ground to watch the exciting miniature air show.

As each plane took off, the audience would suck in its

breath and hold it until the plane was safely in the air. Not all takeoffs and landings were perfect and sometimes a plane would lose control and come crashing to the ground, destroying itself. They were certainly more than toys. A lady sitting next to me said they cost their owners between 300 and 1000 dollars. I saw no children flying there, only grown men.

On the second landing strip, the V-controlled planes were flying. These were all controlled by a gas engine and a string whereby the flyers stood in the center of the field making the planes perform by manipulating two strings attached to a handle that they held in their hands. Although they weren't free flying like the radio-controlled planes, the expert handlers managed to loop, spin, fly and land them with great skill.

The catering wagons had pulled up and parked among the cars, doing, I noticed, a landslide business of hot dogs and cokes. The people there had come to spend the day in this open field, under the hot sun, listening to the drone of motors. It was obvious that model airplane fever was running hot in their blood. I had always considered them toys, not to be taken seriously.

We walked over to a third landing field, and this was where I belonged. Stephen's plane had cost no more than a couple of dollars, but it had taken him days to put it together. Hundreds of tiny pieces of wood had been painstakingly glued, fragile tissue paper was placed over the wings, with a tiny motor and propeller attached to the front of the plane.

Janice Ruth Anchell

Kelvin's flight was successful, perhaps because he had done this many times before. Stephen wasn't as fortunate.

First, the motor didn't run properly. On their knees, the boys soon corrected what was wrong. Then in flight, it suddenly took a spin and crashed, tearing away the tailpiece from the body. I turned away, unable to look at Stephen's face, which I knew would be one of disappointment and sorrow. I need not have bothered because when I did look, he was busily gathering up his tools: masking tape, wire, and glue and rushing to the scene of the crash. Reclaiming his plane, he quickly began making repairs with loving care. Again, his plane took to the air, this time doing a tailspin and losing a wing. More repairs and I wondered how much more this plane, put together with spit and glue, could take, but once more, it took to the air, beautifully this time.

Such smiles, and back slaps and cries of "Look at her go," and "Did you see that?" Completely oblivious except to the lovely soaring thing in the air, we put our hand over our eyes to shield them from the sun and watched the strong-hearted little plane make a perfect landing.

So, the roast was a little overdone, and I had to stay up late to finish the minutes of the next day's meeting, but the glimpse I had into this other world made the stolen hours worthwhile. We had spent almost an entire day flying planes, and I'd very much like to do it again. Would you like to come with us next Sunday? We shouldn't be gone more than half an hour.

The Ride

"Hold on a minute," Charles' voice was startled, "This airport's deserted; there isn't a soul anywhere."

The cab driver spoke for the first time since he'd picked up his passengers ten miles back from an exclusive resort hotel, "Senor, today the Mexican Airlines call a strike, no more planes till the strike is over."

"For crying out loud!" bellowed Ken Monroe, "What did you bring us all the way out here for? Couldn't you have told us back in town?"

"*Senor,* you didn't ask me."

The taxicab was occupied by two well-dressed couples on their way back home after a two-week vacation in a remote resort on the coast of Mexico. Ken Monroe had just finished remarking what a wonderful trip it had been. He was addressing his wife, Alice, and the other couple, Charles and Linda Brown. Now, after this unexpected revelation, everyone started speaking at once.

"Oh Charles, what are we going to do?" asked Linda.

"I don't know, but I've definitely got to be back in Terre Haute by Monday." He turned to the Browns, "I'm trying an important tax case, and my client stands to lose thousands, go to prison, or both if I'm not there."

"Maybe we can get a bus to Mexico City, then I'm sure we can get on a plane from the states there," suggested

Linda.

"Are you kidding?" asked Ken, "It's almost two hundred miles to Mexico City from here and over mountains. Have you seen those Mexican buses? They look like they're held together by chicken wire."

"We've got to do something Ken, the children will be home from camp Monday, and no one will be there," said Alice, who started to cry.

"Ken," Charles said, "there just isn't any other way out of here except by bus or plane, and it's obvious to me the plane's out."

"We'll be taking a heck of a chance, but *c'est le guerre* as they say in Terre Haute; it's worth a try. If everyone's agreed, we'll try the bus."

They all nodded in agreement and in a cloud of dust, the brilliantly home-painted, yellow, and black taxi turned around and started back to town.

At the bus station, they stood in line among their many suitcases and souvenirs that seemed to have multiplied since they were loaded into the cab earlier. Linda clutched the head of a man carved from a coconut shell, its round marble eyes staring into space. She had playfully placed one of the many straw hats she was taking home on her head; over her shoulders was a serape. She, like her husband Charles, was in her early thirties. An easy-going, happy person with a sense of humor.

She was actually looking forward to the misadventure. Charles was a rising young attorney who specialized in tax cases. He liked everything he planned to go off as scheduled and was perturbed at the latest development, but he had accepted it as inevitable that this was the only way he could get back to Terre Haute by Monday and to his client. If Charles Brown told someone he was going to do something, he did it.

The Monroes were in their late forties. Ken ran a successful trucking line in Indiana and was very affluent in certain circles back home. His wife was a well-known club woman, definitely not the adventurous type. Only the thought of her children coming home to an empty house could have made her make this bus trip. She definitely preferred comfort, and her comfort was the great indoors. This was her first trip to a foreign country, and it had taken a great deal of persuasion to make her leave the United States, even for two weeks.

The four stood looking at the small rickety blue bus being loaded for the trip to Mexico City. Coops of chickens had been tied to its roof, along with straw baskets, boxes filled with fruit and vegetables, cords of wood, woven straw purses and hats, all to be sold at the market in the big city. Ken estimated the bus to be at least fifteen years old. It was badly in need of a new paint job.

Ken kicked the tires, "By golly, I don't know that I'd send a truck of mine out with tires like that."

They had no time to comment on this comforting observation since the bus driver began honking his horn, which meant for everyone to get aboard. Alice clutched her jewelry case and overnight bag and followed Linda up the stairs, the two men behind her. They were pushed to the rear of the bus and sat down next to a young man holding a pig and an old woman with a goose that was unhappily honking, rivaling the bus horn. Up above on a shelf was a cage with a green and orange parrot squawking, "*Hola Pepe, que sabe?*"

With a roar and much groaning, the motor sputtered and turned over, and at last they were on their way. They went weaving through the streets of the coastal resort past the luxury hotel they had left a few hours before.

"Boy, if that stuffed shirt *maître d* could see us now," remarked Ken, "I'd bet he'd return my tips."

They all laughed at their ludicrous situation. Two weeks spent around the swimming pool, in the cocktail lounge, dancing, eating gourmet food three times a day, and being pampered by everyone was a far cry from an old broken-down bus surrounded by clucking chickens, a squealing pig, and a squawking parrot.

The first twenty miles were uneventful, with the only noise the sound of the motor and an occasional animal. Just as they had begun to feel settled, they rounded a curve and came to a screeching halt in front of a long oblong building with a thatched roof. A porch ran the length of the structure, with four or five tables and chairs placed around them. From inside, a jukebox or radio blared a Mexican song. The only thing that identified it was a rusted sign that read, "*Tome Coca Cola.*" After everyone left the bus, Charles asked the driver why they had stopped.

He replied, "It is a bus stop, senor, like they have in the

Estados Unidos. Besides, my brother runs this place."

The jukebox blared on, and the four Americans waited patiently on the bus. They all agreed it had been a hectic morning, but at least they were on their way. Thirty minutes later, everyone climbed back into the bus, and once more they were off.

The further they went into the interior, away from the coastal breezes, the warmer it began to get. Ken and Charles had removed their suit coats and loosened their ties. Alice and Linda were fanning themselves with a straw hat. Before they reached the next town, they stopped four more times to pick up passengers that waved to them from the side of the road. Where they came from was a mystery. There were no houses along the road. The people just appeared from the tropical undergrowth that grew as far as the eye could see.

The bus pulled into the square of a tiny Mexican village. The four Americans left the bus to look for a drink of water. In the village, there was one pump that served the seven hundred inhabitants. They dared not drink the water for fear of dysentery, or tourista, as visitors to the country had named it. A simple thing like a drink of water could become a major catastrophe. The only thing they dared drink was bottled water. In the cafe was a huge glass jar of lemonade, with floating green algae instead of ice. Several common drinking glasses were used by all. The only thing available was a bottle of very warm coke.

Alice began to weep "Oh, why did I ever let you talk me into coming to this god-forsaken country. It's all your fault," and she ran back to the bus.

Ken followed after her, and could be heard saying, "Now honey, everything's going to be alright."

Linda left Charles and went up to a woman standing beside one of the many huts made of mud. "*Buenos dias*, senora," one of the few things she remembered from high school Spanish.

The woman motioned her inside. The floor was dirt, there was a table in the corner, several chairs, and there were five woven hammocks swinging from the mud walls. There was no other furniture. Linda accepted a chair. Several ducks and a pig brushed by her expensive patent leather shoes, but Linda seemed not to notice. She was as gracious as possible with her limited vocabulary, and certainly seemed as much at ease as she would have were she visiting a friend in Terre Haute. Little children appeared at the door, staring at her as if she was some great curiosity.

Charles, finding himself alone, had walked to the end of the town, a matter of a few blocks, and found it good to stretch his legs. He heard someone say, "Pssst." Turning, he saw a boy about eight years old. His heart melted, one thing he could not resist was a raggedy child. The boy motioned for him to follow him into the alley.

He looked at Charles with big luminous, brown eyes from a tiny, pinched face and said, "Senor, I have a sister, only ten pesos."

"Oh my god," moaned Charles, and he felt sick. This pathetic little boy procuring for his sister was just too much. "*No niño*, but this is for you," he reached into his pocket and gave the child all his loose change.

Once more, the bus was honking for its passengers, everyone ran towards it, and they were off again.

Kenneth was the first to speak, "After you left and Alice started feeling better, I thought I'd look around a bit. You won't believe me, but I went into their market, and they had meat hanging from the ceiling, every piece of it covered with flies, and people were buying it. They were selling the entrails. I tried to take a picture, but some big guy threw a tomato at me. It just about ruined my shirt. It's hard to believe people could live like that."

Alice, who was sitting huddled down in the seat, said, "If I ever get back to Indiana, nothing will ever get me to leave again."

"You know," continued Ken, "we left on this bus at 9:30, and it's 1:00 now, and we aren't one-third the way. There isn't any schedule that I can make out; they just stop and go as they please. I can just imagine what would happen if I ran my truck line this way."

The blowout sounded like a gunshot, and even the most jaded of the passengers screamed or gasped until the bus came to a halt. The Mexicans began to leave the bus without being told, obviously accustomed to whatever had happened.

"I knew it. I knew those tires were bad," remarked Ken, "No self-respecting person in the states would ride on tires like that."

"I'll never get home; I just know I won't," and Alice's tears began anew.

Several of the men, among them Charles, began to replace the tire with a spare. The rest of the passengers sat or squatted beside the roadside, visiting and eating much like they were on a picnic—unconcerned, unhurried, seemingly without a care in the world.

Linda left the group and walked down by a bridge she saw in the distance. There, by a stream, were some half-dozen women, naked to the waist, kneeling beside a stream doing their washing. She went down among them, took several packages of gum from her purse, and offered them to the half-clothed children. Unlike their mothers, the children all had on shirts but nothing below the waist. Linda had begun to get used to this; all the children in the village had been dressed the same way. A little girl of three or four climbed into her lap and fingered the pearl choker around her neck. She sat there watching the women, who whispered and stared and giggled at her presence.

Soon Charles came to tell her the bus was ready to leave. "Charles, I didn't know Mexico was like this. All I've seen in the past two weeks were luxurious hotels and adorable little shops. Now I see poverty and deprivation everywhere."

"Just because they don't have hot and cold running water and toilets like you doesn't mean they're deprived or impoverished. They certainly look happier than we do. You don't see anyone among them worrying about payments on a car or house or a client fighting a tax case."

Linda sighed, "I suppose you're right, but I need to think about it. It's all so different from Terre Haute."

Three breakdowns and one flat tire later, the bus limped into the capital of Mexico. It was almost midnight. They had been traveling for fourteen hours. Wild-eyed, disheveled, and tired, they took a taxi to the nearest hotel, only to find there were no vacancies.

"This is a heck of a country," said Ken. "Lousy buses, rotten roads, food you can't eat, water you can't drink, and now no place to stay."

At last, they found a hotel. It had one room available. A suite, the Presidential Suite, a penthouse, which came with a bar and a valet, at $100.00 a night. They were too tired to argue or look further.

From the ridiculous bus to the sublime room came the four weary people. Alice collapsed on the bed, a cold towel on her head. Her husband, Ken, poured himself a stiff drink and turned on the T.V. Charles was on the phone calling the airlines for reservations, and Linda stood on the balcony of the penthouse, looking out over the city. She had been in another world today, and it was too soon to understand the significance of what she had seen. But she already knew that never again would she take her carpeted floors, the water from the faucet, the flick of a switch that turns on electricity for granted. She had almost missed really seeing the heart of the country. She wondered how many other things she had missed.

The Paradox

Just before the lights dimmed for the first act, Mary Anders looked up from her theater program and saw Eloise Gill across the aisle. The last time Mary had seen Eloise was on vacation a month ago in Acapulco. During intermission, when the crowd surged from their seats to the lobby, Mary followed Eloise up the aisle.

Anticipating a gleeful reunion with Eloise, Mary was puzzled when she received a definite rebuff. It wasn't until Eloise introduced her escort pointedly as her fiancé that it became clear to Mary the sudden change in Eloise's personality, for in Acapulco, Eloise had been with her husband, and the man at her side was definitely not the same person.

Everyone on the plane flying to Mexico had been keenly aware of Eloise. After takeoff, Eloise left her seat and made friends with all the passengers. She was introducing strangers to other strangers and spoon-whipped up a feeling of gaiety and camaraderie that Mary had never experienced on a plane. Mary wished she could be a little more extroverted; she found it very difficult to make friends with strangers.

The hotel the travel agency had selected for Mary was unique in that apart from the main building were many tiny, pink, stucco cottages—all on a hill, each with its own swimming pool. Each cottage had a balcony that over-looked the magnificent Acapulco harbor. The setting was romantic, and it was there Mary planned to spend most of her time quietly reading and resting.

Stepping onto her balcony to admire the view, she had recognized Eloise, the girl on the plane. She and her husband had the cottage below hers and were swimming in their pool. Eloise saw Mary and sent a friendly wave in her direction. A twinge of envy that couldn't be suppressed passed through Mary. She had a wonderful job as an executive secretary but had yet to meet the man she wanted to spend the rest of her life with. The only time she felt discontented was when she saw such obviously happy couples as Eloise and her husband.

Several days later, Mary was among the hotel guests having a solitary drink before dinner.

In swept Eloise on her husband's arm. "This is ridiculous," she cried, "we're all here for a fun time." The sprinkling of people looked startled when she continued, "Come on everyone, pull your chairs up. Let's get together."

Obediently, everyone pulled their chairs together, even the reluctant Mary, who would have liked to be left alone. She was too shy and insecure within herself to like meeting strangers. They were all being forced into friendliness whether they liked it or not. Shortly, the whispering and occasional clink of glasses were replaced by much gaiety and laughter.

Eloise went further and had the waiters push the tables

together in the dining room, and the conviviality continued through dinner. Mary ceased being resentful at having her privacy invaded. You couldn't resist Eloise; she was so effervescent and seemed genuinely interested in everyone. If only she could be as easy and natural with people, Mary thought, feeling envy once again.

Eloise continued to be the lifeblood of the hotel. It was she who water skied and scuba-dived and talked everyone into trying it with her. It was the consensus of opinion by all that met her that their vacation had been made more meaningful by coming into contact with her. It was a very happy group whenever Eloise was around, and Mary was one of the fascinated followers.

During all this time, Eloise's husband stayed at her side, seemingly devoted and attentive. Each evening the two would swim in their pool, and Mary would watch and wish she might trade places with Eloise. Envy was a new emotion for Mary; she had been quite content with her unmarried state until this trip.

Eloise and her husband left Acapulco several days before Mary. A farewell dinner was held, and each guest toasted the couple with many compliments. Towards the end of the evening, Eloise left the table, tears streaming down her face. This was interpreted as regret at leaving all her friends.

Now, Mary knew better; there must have been many other reasons. This face-to-face confrontation at the theater with Eloise and her fiancé had been embarrassing for both of them. Mary was happy to return to her seat and have the lights dimmed for the second act.

The next few months found Mary thinking of little else except Eloise and her lover. The girl had been an absolute fraud, a charlatan. She was fascinated at having been a witness to an illicit affair. Of course, she had read about similar affairs in books and seen them in the movies, but a ringside seat at one she had never anticipated. This couple hadn't been furtive or secret, but right out in the open, and only by accident had they been discovered. Her final conclusion was that no harm had been done. She was certain Eloise Gill was not the girl's real name.

The next year, the travel agency suggested Aspen as her vacation spot. The day she arrived, she went to the ski course and was fitted with all the correct equipment. That evening, sitting around the great fire in the lodge, watching all the many happy couples, a man whom she recognized as one of the ski instructors sat down beside her.

"You seem to be all alone; may I join you?" he asked.

Her usual reply would have been to ignore the man, bolt from the room, indignant at not having a proper introduction. This was precisely what her mother had taught her to do. Instead, her heartbeat faster, and she said, "Yes, please do; by the way, I didn't catch your name. Mine is Eloise."

The Great Adventure

He had always been called Little Eddie by everyone that knew him, and he hated that nickname with a passion. Perhaps being called "little" wouldn't have bothered an ordinary man, but Eddie had just celebrated his twenty-fifth birthday, and although he was a man, he stood but five foot four. To him, the nickname was not one of endearment or friendliness; rather, it seemed to be one of derision.

He had been a presser in a cleaning shop since he graduated from high school. His father had abandoned his mother before Eddie was born and had never bothered to look him up again. From the wedding picture his mom had kept, he could see where his short stature came from. He forgave his father for the years of deprivation he and his mom had gone through and the indignity of being on relief for years, but the one thing he could not forgive was the stature he had inherited.

Except for height, he looked like any ordinary brown-eyed, sandy-haired youth and seemed to be perfectly content with himself and his job in the cleaning shop. But after his mother died, he became dissatisfied and terribly lonely. The two had always been very close. Always, after the weekly rent was paid, there would be a little money left, and they would take off for the local movie house like a couple of kids. Their favorite show was always a good

Western. Without her, it just wasn't the same.

He thought he would go out of his mind missing her until he developed a plan that gave him direction and purpose. He wanted to go across the United States on a horse. Why a horse? Why not a bus or a train? Not only had the Western movies influenced him, but he found on the infrequent times he had ridden a horse rented from the local stables that no one could see how short he was, and he felt like a man for one of the few times in his adult life.

He told no one of his ambition because he knew they would think him crazy. As a boy, he had spent many hours in the library, and he yearned not only for the feel of manliness he had when mounted on a horse but also to see the wonders he had read about. So, he kept his dream to himself and made plans.

He carefully figured that with one thousand dollars, he could make it from one coast to the other. This included buying a horse, saddle, and a gun for protection and paying for the food he and his horse would need. He had a notebook filled with pages of maps and possible routes he and his horse would take. His afternoon off from the cleaning shop was Thursday, and each week found him outside the city at the auction pen, looking at the horses, trying to find out as much about them as he could. In the back of his mind was the possibility of finding just what he wanted, which was a cross between a black horse and a tall buckskin that carried two of his favorite movie stars. He envisioned himself riding across the plains as they did.

Getting the thousand dollars was another thing, for his

salary as a presser was barely adequate to support him. He saved pennies by doing without everything but the barest necessities. The pennies and nickels placed in a small fruit jar, and when there were enough to make a dollar, he stopped by the bank and changed them for a crisp, new dollar bill. The dollar bill was then placed in a little tin box under his bed. Each night he counted his money, almost as if by doing so, it multiplied and grew. He was not above looking for empty soda bottles thrown there by passersby. These brought him two cents, and if he were lucky, occasionally, he found a bottle that brought him a nickel. He saved paper, tying it carefully in neat bundles, then when he had a full load would borrow a neighbor's wheelbarrow and push it six miles to a place that bought old rags and used papers. Nothing was too demeaning that helped fill the jar with money and bring the dream closer.

One Thursday at the auction pen, he made friends with a man he had seen there quite often. There seemed to be nothing this new acquaintance didn't know about horses, and Eddie was very impressed.

It was unusual for Eddie to take up with a stranger; he always stayed very much to himself. But this man was so understanding it wasn't long before Eddie found himself confiding his dream. When the man didn't laugh at him, Eddie told him all about the maps, the money, and the struggle he was going through to make his plans come true. To himself, Eddie wished he had had a father that resembled this tall, strong-looking, virile man. When the stranger suggested that Eddie come over to a hotel room and talk some more, Eddie couldn't have been happier.

The next day Eddie failed to appear for work. This was unusual, for Eddie had rarely missed a day at the cleaning shop. It was Friday, and the owner found himself in a bind without his presser, and by closing time, he had made up his mind to let Eddie go. On the way home, he decided to stop by Eddie's house and tell him he wouldn't be needed anymore.

He hadn't realized how poor Eddie was until he approached a little unpainted shack in a row of other unpainted shacks beside the railroad tracks. He was surprised to see so many people outside in the yard and even a police car. Maybe the kid was in trouble, he thought, and he pushed past the people into the house.

"What's happened here?" he asked the officer. "I'm Little Eddie's boss."

"Haven't you heard? It's been on every radio newscast today. They found Little Eddie this morning dead in a hotel room over near the auction pen. A brutal sex crime. Looks like he tried to resist, but the other guy was too strong. We've found a box full of new one-dollar bills under Little Eddie's bed and a notebook labeled 'The Great Adventure.' Can't make heads or tails out of the notebook, just a bunch of crazy maps. Wonder where the kid got all that money?"

Myrna

Myrna Jones was in a state of panic. She couldn't believe it was true. In three months, Billy Joe was actually coming to see her. They had been corresponding for two years but had never met. His picture had been in the paper, a pensive, lonely-looking sailor stationed in Alaska. He had written to the editor, giving his name and address, asking for a girl to write to him.

Myrna had responded at once, making the excuse to herself that she was being patriotic since he was in the service. The truth was, she was lonely too, a girl of eighteen who weighed over 185 pounds since she was thirteen and never had a date.

The correspondence had started politely and reservedly. This was a new experience because she had never written to a boy. In fact, she knew very little about the male species. When she was three, she had lost her father in a railroad accident. With great effort, her mother had brought her up, working as a cleaning woman in different office buildings. When Myrna graduated from high school, she took a six-week secretarial course, all they could afford.

Although she did everything the employment agency told her–neat and clean, wearing a simple dark dress, hair neatly combed–she was never hired for the job she wanted. She knew it was her weight, and there were times when she would attempt to diet, but her tremendous loneliness always drove her back to the ice cream counter, where mounds of hot fudge and ice cream were her only solace.

She finally was hired to do office work for an auto parts store. Her desk was in the back of an old warehouse, set apart by a partition. A very unglamorous and dull place, but at least she was getting a paycheck and helped contribute to the household.

Her letters to the sailor continued on a very formal plane for six more months. One day Billy Joe changed "Sincerely Yours" to "With Love." She returned with "All My Love" instead of "Yours Truly." After that, there was no more pretense. They were no longer writing letters; they were writing letters of love.

After two years, even "All My Love" had long ago been dropped for more personal, more endearing terms. They had poured their hearts out to one another, their dreams, ambitions, and hopes. He was a boy from Oklahoma, his first time away from home. His mother and father were divorced, and he had been brought up by his father. Billy Joe admired his dad and wanted very much to follow in his footsteps. It was the reason he was saving his money to buy his own cab when he was dismissed from the Navy.

Many times, he had asked her for a picture, but she managed to ignore his request, always putting him off, promising to send it another time.

His tour of duty was over, and he was coming to see her in three months. She was more perturbed than she had ever been over anything in her life. Writing letters to a boy was one thing; being with him in the flesh was another. She knew the minute he laid eyes on her, he would wish they had never met. They would look like Jack Spratt and his wife. She couldn't bear the thought of his embarrassment.

Her agony and torture were finally relieved when she decided she must lose weight. There was no other way out. She became as resolute as a piece of steel, putting herself on a high protein diet, and not once going near the candy and pastries where she had always found solace and comfort. Slowly but surely, her avoirdupois melted away, and she began to emerge like a butterfly from its cocoon.

She had her hair styled and bought several new dresses, and for the first time in her life, she was invited out by a salesman that had been calling on her boss for a year. This was the first time he had ever noticed her. However, she refused his invitation, wanting to wait for Billy Joe.

She had been one of the many pretty-faced fat girls seen so often. Now that her cheekbones were exposed for the first time, she was beautiful. This new image, this self she never knew existed, frightened and delighted her at the same time. The fright because she had no experience with men. She marveled at her newfound appearance. Before it had taken her no more than ten minutes to dress, the time had been extended to one hour.

An electric current began to appear between Myrna's and Billy Joe's letters. Excited about their meeting that was drawing near, both expressed doubts and wrote, "What if you don't like me?" to which they answered with reassuring notes.

Myrna spent days preparing for their first meeting. No detail was left undone. She even passed up the polka dot and printed dresses she had always worn for a simple, sophisticated blue linen that matched her eyes. When she was completely dressed, she stepped back and looked at herself in the mirror and was pleased by what she saw.

Billy Joe was just like his photograph, a slight boy with light brown hair. He was just the way she imagined he would be, very quiet and shy. She was so glad that she had not run from her problem but had faced it head on. She was a woman any man would be proud to know. At least she had a chance with him now. Myrna loved him at once, all her motherly instincts yearning to give him the love he had never had.

She spent a sleepless night after they parted, excited with plans for the future. In the morning, her mother awakened her and handed her a special delivery letter. It was from Billy Joe.

He wrote:

My Dearest One,

You are more than I ever had the right to expect; I cannot ask anyone as lovely as you to be my wife. I am not worthy. I am taking the next bus to Oklahoma. I shall always love you.

Yours Forever,
Billy Joe

"What have I done?" she cried. "In heaven's name, I've

frightened him away." She dressed quickly, knowing what she must do.

As she started out the front door, her mother shouted, "Where are you going? It's Sunday."

"First to the bus station to buy a ticket to Oklahoma, then to the drugstore for a double malted, a chocolate soda, and a banana split for a starter, then I'm coming home for breakfast to write to Billy Joe."

When she was almost to the corner, she turned and shouted back at her mother, "Make that a big stack of pancakes and some French toast; I've got a long way to go in a hurry."

Skippy, the Dog Who Lived in an Apartment

Skippy was a wire-haired terrier that had lived all his life in an apartment building high above the streets. Today was Saturday, his very favorite day because his entire family almost always stayed home with him. He should have been happy, but instead, he lay sadly under the coffee table, his mournful eyes following the movements of the three people he loved most, Bobby his twelve-year-old master and Bobby's parents, Isobel and Murray.

They were all getting dressed, not Saturday-morning-stay-at-home dressed but going out-special dressed.

Skippy knew that when Isobel picked up her purse and put on her gloves and Murray tied a tie around his neck that they were going out somewhere. Going out! Leaving! His heart gave a thump that put a lump in his throat. They couldn't do that; he'd been home alone every day that week. Didn't they know how lonely it could be for hours on end with nothing to do but stare at the walls? After all, how long could you amuse yourself chewing on a rubber bone or chasing a rolling ball around? Skippy knew they wouldn't be taking him along; they never did.

He was slightly larger than the poodles he always saw accompanying their masters, just enough to make him too heavy to carry and much too strong to be restrained on a leash. The only time he ever left home was when Bobby took him around the block in the morning and again in the evening. All he'd ever really seen were sidewalks and elevators.

Now, today they were leaving him again. It just wasn't fair; he had waited all week for this day. Skippy held his head a little lower between his paws. As the three of them walked past him, they all stopped to pat his head and tell him to be a good dog. Isobel put out a bowl of fresh water and some dog food. Who could eat, he thought, when they were being left all alone? He turned his face away. To show just how upset he was, he didn't lick their hands or wag his tail; he just lay quietly and pretended not to care. As they closed the door behind them and Skippy realized that all hope was gone that they might change their minds, the telephone rang.

Bobby's mother returned to answer it, holding her hand over the receiver, she turned to Murray and said, "It's the Smiths. They want us to bring Skippy." At the sound of his name, Skippy sat up.

"I don't think so, Isobel; he's not accustomed to being out; he won't know how to act."

"Please, Dad," Bobby pleaded, "I'll watch him every minute, you'll see."

"They do have a nice backyard, and it's fenced," added Isobel.

Murray looked down at the three anxious faces and said, "Well, all right, we'll try it just this once."

Skippy felt his leash snap onto his collar, the door closed

behind him, and he felt so happy he wiggled from the top of his head to the tip of his stubby tail. He was to be with his family for the entire day after all and away from that dreaded apartment.

It was quite a long ride and Skippy soon tired of looking out the car window and snuggled into Bobby's lap. At least part of him snuggled; the rest of him was just too big for Bobby to hold.

The first thing Bobby's mother did when they arrived at the Smiths was to tell Bobby to take Skippy to the backyard.

"Backyard? I wonder what that is?" Skippy asked himself.

When he saw it, he couldn't believe his eyes, for surely it must be one of the wonders of the world. There was fresh dirt to dig in, bushes to explore, grass to run on, and trees to rub against. He was so excited he didn't know just where to start, so he ran from one thing to another, faster and faster, letting out small yips of excitement. He and Bobby continued this way until Bobby fell down and tore the knee of his trousers.

"Now stay here, Skippy, and be a good boy; I'll be right back; I'm just going to see if Mother can fix it."

Left alone in the yard, Skippy began to explore a little more thoroughly. Behind the bushes, he dug a hole. How good the earth felt on his paws and nose. He wished he had a backyard, then when his family left for the day, he'd have something more to do than just look at the walls.

Behind a large bush, he found a broken place in the

fence, just big enough for his body. He slipped through, only intending to leave for a minute, when he came face to face with a big, red chow dog.

This wasn't the first time he'd ever seen a dog like this. Only a few weeks before, Bobby had been walking him, and a similar dog had chased them all the way back to the apartment. When they reached their building, they ran in and slammed the glass door behind them, both shivering and shaking from fright.

If Bobby had been afraid of the chow, that was good enough reason for Skippy to be afraid. He started to return through the broken fence into the Smith's backyard, but the chow dog blocked his way. Then the big dog uttered a low growl and started toward Skippy. Skippy began to run in the opposite direction, and he ran and ran as fast as he could go, only occasionally looking behind him to see the other dog in hot pursuit.

At last, he lost the chow and stopped behind a big brick wall to rest. As soon as he was rested, he would return to the Smith's house. He hoped Bobby hadn't missed him. He was sorry he had disobeyed and left the backyard.

Finding the Smith's house turned out to be more difficult than he had thought. He was in a strange neighborhood, and all the houses looked alike. It wasn't until it became dark that Skippy was ready to acknowledge that he was lost. Finally, he lay down to sleep and, for the first time since he'd been born, went without his supper. He thought about his family and hoped they weren't too worried. He dreamed that they were calling him, but he couldn't answer. It was a very disturbing dream, and he was glad when he woke up.

The next morning the hunger pains were very real, and Skippy started off to find something to eat. He wished Bobby's mother were here to feed him, she might leave him alone in the apartment, but one thing she never did was forget to feed him.

Down the alley he went until his nose caught the aroma of food. He instinctively decided the wonderful smell was coming from a garbage can. Skippy stood on his hind feet, the better to see into the can when suddenly it toppled over, and the garbage went spilling every which way.

The back door of the house opened, and a big woman carrying a broom came running out the door. She was screaming at Skippy and waving the broom in the air. She managed to hit him just once with the broom, and Skippy let out a loud yelp that he'd never heard before. He was more frightened than when he'd been running from the chow dog. This time without even looking back, he ran until he was exhausted.

At noontime, he began walking again, so hungry he didn't know what to do. Oh, how he wished he had eaten the bowl of food Bobby's mother had offered him the day before. Perhaps then he wouldn't feel so empty.

Down the street he walked, head slumped down between his shoulders; he was so lost. He hoped they'd find him soon. It was then he saw a big, black cat eating something from a bowl. Skippy edged a little closer; perhaps she would be charitable and share whatever she had. He wasn't too familiar with cats, and he was quite surprised when it raised its back, spat at him, and reached for his face with its claws. Skippy cried out and once more went running down the street.

He was completely disheartened and ready to give up when a little girl approached and said, "Here, doggie, want to play?"

She threw out a ball, and he retrieved it for her. This was a game he knew well. Bobby would play it with him for hours on Saturday. The little girl had a sack of cookies and offered one to Skippy. He was grateful, and for the first time since early that morning, his stomach ceased to hurt.

Afterward, the little girl turned and began walking homeward. Skippy followed close behind her. After all, hers had been the first kindness he'd felt since that fateful minute he had walked through the broken fence.

When they arrived at the little girl's house, Skippy stayed back on the edge of the sidewalk, afraid to follow her up on the porch. Surely enough, he heard the mother scold the little girl for allowing another dog to follow her home. They shut the door behind them, and once more, Skippy was all alone. He lay down beside the porch and fell asleep.

Later, after it was dark, the door of the house opened, and the mother exclaimed, "That dog is still here. I wonder whom he belongs to?"

She whistled softly and called gently to Skippy, who came to her and sat looking up while she knelt to examine his dog tags. Those tags, he'd always hated them because they disturbed his sleep by jangling when he turned over.

Now, he was grateful for them because he heard the woman say, "His name is Skippy, and here is his phone number. Now, Skippy, you stay right there and don't leave." With that, she went back into the house.

Skippy waited what seemed to him a long time in the dark. He worried that maybe his family wouldn't come to get him. He feared he might have wandered too far away for them to come after him. What if they were angry with him for leaving? After all, he should have obeyed Bobby and stayed in the yard. Then there was Bobby's mother and dad; they might never take him out again. After all, why should they? He most certainly had not proved obedient and trustworthy but instead had caused them extra trouble. Perhaps it would be best if he just left and didn't bother them anymore.

He stood up on his feet, shivered a moment in the cold night air, and started walking away. Minutes later, when he was halfway down the block, he heard a car drive up. It was them, his family; what should he do?

He heard the lady of the house say, "But he was just here a minute ago. I don't know where he went."

Then Bobby's mother said, "It's all our fault, we never take him out, and he doesn't know how to act when he gets out."

"Isobel, Bobby, I promise you that if we find him, we'll take him with us more often. A dog like that shouldn't be confined to an apartment every day."

Then Bobby began calling his name in a small, choked

voice, as if he were trying not to cry, "Skip, please come here; I promise never to leave you alone outside again."

They began walking towards Skippy, who was all but invisible in the darkness. He ran and jumped into Bobby's arms, almost knocking him over. His entire body wiggled in joy at being found. They all took turns holding him, each one giving him a special squeeze.

They thanked the lady who called them and started the long drive back home in the car. The familiar hum of the elevator going up was music to Skippy's ears; the walls of the apartment had never looked so good. After a good warm meal, Skippy lay down under the coffee table, completely worn out. All those other dogs, he thought before he fell asleep, let them have the perils of a backyard; he'd take the security of an apartment house any day.

The Party

Harry McDermott had just been promoted to Vice-President in Charge of Credit at the I.C. Bliss Company, maker of the famous Ticky-Tacky Doll. He should have been all aglow with his rising success, but instead, he was in a state of apprehension. For it was customary at I.C. Bliss and Company for anyone who was promoted to give a dinner party for the rest of the staff, and Harry was in no position to do so.

Emily, his wife, had long ago sworn never to give another party. It made her nervous having him figure out how much each guest would eat if they had two and one-half drinks, one and one-half helpings of the meat course, and if one-third refused dessert because they were on a diet.

Harry wasn't exactly a tightwad nor miserly; he only seemed to be. He was an accountant, and from force of habit, he reduced everything he saw to a set of figures. A new suit was not blue and fit well; rather, it cost sixty dollars, and if worn for three years, twice per week would cost nineteen cents per wearing. A cup of coffee five times per week was not a hot beverage to relax with during an afternoon break but was ten cents plus a tip for the waitress, which, when divided by the cost of a pound of coffee, gave him how much coffee he could buy if he forwent the coffee break and drank it at home. Not that he would go so far as to give up the coffee, he just liked to see everything in numbers. It was so much neater.

Sunset was a signal for him to get out his watch and count the minutes and seconds it took for it to go down. Lately, he had been finding beauty in columns and numbers, especially in his bankbook, and he loved to watch the balance grow from month to month.

His wife was firm about the party. It was only after an evening of persuasion that she finally consented to have it, and then only after Harry promised to let her plan and execute it by herself, with no questions asked or advice offered. Harry, whose reputation at the office was at stake, agreed to her terms. He had no alternative.

Having been given carte blanche, Emily, who truly loved giving a party, was ecstatic and set about planning menus and flower arrangements. She was like a prisoner seeing the sunshine or a dog let loose in a meat factory. She went all the way. This would be a grand dinner, and it should be. After all, Harry wasn't promoted every day.

She ordered American Beauty Roses as a centerpiece for her table and the best prime rib roast from the butcher. The bakery was instructed to make a special order of tiny cakes just for the occasion. It had been a long time since she had given a party, and she intended to do it in style. She was very careful not to tell Harry of her plans, for he was certain to make everything into equations.

Several days before the event, Harry was looking through a sheaf of papers, searching for their last month's electric bill, which he wanted to compare to the present one. Accidentally, he came upon the list his wife had made for the party. As he read it, he became a little weak, for he knew what prime rib cost a pound and how much that little French bakery charged for special orders. If Emily, who had certainly been carried away, were allowed to continue, the party would come to over $5.00 per person, which was a ridiculous figure. Besides, there would be nothing to add to the bank balance this month. He quickly copied Emily's list and returned hers to the desk.

That afternoon he visited the various stores and changed each order. The roast from prime to choice; the specially ordered cakes to what they had in stock; the roses to chrysanthemums. Now the party was closer to $2.50 per person, a much more realistic figure. By the time Emily received the items, it would be too late to do anything about it. Later, he would convince her he had done the right thing.

The night of the party, Harry rushed home from work and dashed up the stairs to dress. Emily followed him, lovely and radiant in a long hostess gown, partially covered by an organza apron.

"Hurry, Harry; I want you to see everything before the guests arrive."

He put his head down, and she kissed him on the cheek before vanishing to the kitchen. Quickly showering and shaving, Harry put on cologne that came in a two-ounce bottle. He calculated that by using it twice a day for a month, it cost five cents each time. He was humming a little tune, pleased that Emily had not been angry with the changes he had made. The entire office had been excited about coming to his house; the girls especially had been talking about nothing else for days.

Coming down the stairs, he had the frightening feeling that something was amiss. It was beautiful, resplendent with white linen, crystal, and polished silver. A vase stood in the center, but with no flowers, only a piece of paper protruding from its yawning mouth.

"Emily, where are the flowers?" he asked. "Haven't they come?"

"Oh, they sent the wrong thing, so I sent them back."

He picked the piece of paper from the vase and read: there should have been long-stemmed American Beauty roses here, sorry. Harry rushed into the kitchen and in horror saw it clean and sterile. He opened the oven door and breathed a sigh of relief. It was all right. The roasting pan was there. He picked up the potholder and removed the lid. He needn't have bothered. The pan was ice cold and contained nothing but a note. He read: I was to have prime rib roast.

"Emily, what have you done? How could you embarrass me like this? The guests will be here any minute. How can I face them?"

"The same way I'm going to face the florist, the butcher,

and the baker. What kind of ninny do you think has a husband who cancels all her orders?"

"Emily, I didn't think you'd mind. Forgive me. I'm sorry. Please help me out."

There was a loud shrill sound as the doorbell rang.

"Emily, please." He was white-faced and stricken.

"Don't worry; I've already made reservations at the *Bel de Paese*. Now go open the door." She could hear talking as he crossed the living room to the front door, "If the average person has one and one-half drinks and doesn't order dessert, it might not be so bad."

The Marriage Machine

"Jim, you either convince your ex-wives to accept less alimony, or you'll go to prison for failure to make payments."

James Dawson III, sixty-three years old, dapper, and quite handsome, looked at his accountant in disbelief, "That's out; not one of them is willing to give up the style I accustomed them to."

The two men had been poring over James' books for several hours, adding and subtracting sums on a large sheet of paper.

"I'm the highest-paid engineer at Adams Aircraft, and you're telling me I can't pay my bills?"

The accountant stood up to leave, "Paying alimony to three women is expensive; you simply can't afford them and continue the style of living you're enjoying. Somebody has got to give, and I'm afraid it's you." With that, he picked up his briefcase and left.

James Dawson sat for a few minutes in thought and dialed the telephone, "Helen, honey, this is Jimbo; how's the gal? I heard you've been seeing Al Cortland lately; anything to it?" His voice dropped lower after he listened to her answer, "Oh, I know you're trying, but Helen, those alimony payments are murder. I know I should have thought of that before I married Susan and Alice. It's too late now, so keep in touch, Helen; you're bound to meet someone soon."

He dialed again and repeated the same conversation with Susan. By the time he spoke to Alice, his voice was no longer bright and cheery but glum and despairing. "Alice, I agree it's hard to meet someone right away, but it's been six months since the divorce."

He jumped when she slammed the phone down. He rang for his secretary to come in and be seated and then asked her for help with his problem, "Either my ex-wives get married, or I go broke paying them alimony. Any suggestions?"

"Couldn't you introduce them to some of your friends?"

"I tried that, no good."

"Maybe if they went on a cruise, they might meet someone."

"Too expensive; I can't afford it."

"Mr. Dawson, have you thought of using a computer?"

He gave her a sharp glance.

She continued, "You know the ads in the paper, Matrionics? You give all the information about yourself to a machine, and it comes out with the perfect mate. I see the ad every day in the paper. In fact, that's how Miss Simpkins in personnel found her husband."

Jim jumped to his feet, "Get me the address. Anything is worth a try. Miss Brown, if this works, I'll personally see you get a raise."

When Jim left the office at four, he was whistling for the first time that day. At the Matrionics Bureau, he was given a questionnaire to fill out. Only when he assured the assistant manager that he was best friends with his three ex-wives and that he was doing this on their behalf was he allowed three blank forms that were to be fed to the huge computing machine.

Helen Dawson, he wrote, red hair, green eyes, 5'2", likes horse racing (as a matter of fact, that's where he had met her). Then, Susan Dawson, 5'4", blonde with blue eyes, favorite sport, boxing.

Susan he had met at the matches one night. Boxing he didn't care for but had gone that night for lack of something else to do. When he was married to Susan, they had standing ringside tickets for every match. What a relief it had been when they were divorced, and he could stop going.

Alice Dawson, brunette. When he had first met her, he had thought she was smarter than the other two, at least in a business way. He had met her one afternoon when he had dropped into his stockbrokers. She didn't have any stock; she just sat in front of the big board, making fortunes on paper. It didn't work that way when you were playing for keeps; he had found out after they were married. He divorced her just before she had almost ruined him.

Finished, he handed the papers to the assistant manager, who placed them in the huge machine. After much light flashing and wheel grinding, the monster spit out three pink cards. These were handed to James Dawson in exchange for three ten-dollar bills.

Over a cocktail, he looked at the cards. The first one read Alonzo Matteo: Jockey. That would be for Helen, who liked racing, and he wouldn't be much taller than her. The second one read Harry Hugo: Boxer. James had read of him somewhere in the sports section of the paper. Susan would like that. She had always wanted to know a flesh and blood fighter; well, he was going to give her the chance.

The third card read, Lauren Valentine, Jr.: Stockbroker– a third generation family. Just what Susan needed, maybe he could keep from selecting the wrong stocks–he hoped so. It would be a shame if they went broke.

He planned a party that included the six principals. The evening started out rather badly, what with his three wives together for the time, eyeing one another suspiciously. The three men had nothing in common, but James Dawson had the dinner table set with place cards which necessitated the pairing off of each of the couples according to the computer.

James Dawson sat back and surveyed his handiwork, admiring the coup he had pulled, when suddenly he noticed Helen was no longer with Alonzo Matteo but was with Hugo. Susan was with the stockbroker, and Alice was with the jockey. This would never do, so he intervened and returned the rightful men to the rightful girls. This happened several more times, and the party resembled a fast game of musical chairs. By the end of the evening, James Dawson III was exhausted but happy, for all three of his ex-wives left with the right man.

For the next few months, he received daily reports from Helen, Susan, and Alice. They were having a marvelous time with their jockey, boxer, and stockbroker, respectively. Then the reports became less frequent, and when he did hear from them, they explained that they were too busy to call. He couldn't help but feel 'left out.' After all, he started this whole thing.

By the end of the six months, he began to have serious doubts about what he had done. Maybe he shouldn't have played so fast and loose with fate. The truth was that he already missed them. Dejectedly, he announced to his secretary that he didn't want to be disturbed.

He tried calling his ex-wives, but there was no answer. Before it was too late, he must confess what he had done. They would all have a big laugh over the entire thing, and everything would be as it was in the past.

Later that day, he heard a timid knock and a quiet voice asked permission to enter. Miss Brown handed him a telegram from Las Vegas that read, JUST MARRIED STOP ALIMONY PAYMENTS THANKS A MILLION. It was signed by Helen, Susan, and Alice. Good heavens! They had all eloped together.

It had worked, they were happy, and he was free.

"Now that this is settled, perhaps I can get some work done." He glanced up at Miss Brown and saw her for the first time. He wondered why he hadn't noticed her before. Perhaps she wouldn't be busy tonight. After all, he needed someone to celebrate this occasion with him. Didn't he?

Possessed

I leaned against the iron railing fence and looked out at the street as I had done every day since I'd been there. One of the kids was yelling for me to come play ball, but I couldn't. I had to keep watch. Today might be the day.

Suddenly, I saw her just as I knew I would. She was in a car at the stop light with a man I had never seen before, probably one of my new uncles. She glanced towards "the home," and I waved, but she didn't see me. There was no need to worry because surely, in a minute they'd turn into the driveway, the big iron gate would open, and at last, we would be together again.

The light changed, but instead of turning, the car sped on. Shocked by this turn of events, my head began to whirl, and my heart pounded as if it would burst. Without thinking, I gave a quick thrust and pushed my thin body through the rails of the fence and went running after the car, screaming, "Mother, Mother, please come back!"

I ran faster than I'd ever run before. It was two intersections later, after dodging traffic and people, that I realized the car was lost to me. My legs couldn't continue the pace I'd set, so I slowed down to a walk. Probably she hadn't stopped because the uncle was in a hurry. Maybe she had gone back to our apartment and would take the streetcar back. Rationalizing that as long as I was outside and would be in trouble for leaving, I might as well go on home and save her the long trip back. Home was one room above a cleaning shop. The last place we lived together was somewhere on the other side of the city. I asked directions to Bowker Street and was told it was seven miles to the west. I took a deep breath, straightened my shoulders, and started out to find her.

When my mother left me three months ago, she had promised to come to get me as soon as she could. My dad had died the year before, and she had to start work. His death had no effect on me since he traveled, and I seldom had seen him except occasionally on Sundays. It only disturbed me because now my mother and I had to be separated each day. There was no one to leave me with during the day, and she worried that I would get hurt on the street. Before leaving, she had knelt before me, arms around my waist, and explained that this was a foster home that kept children until their parents could provide for them properly. How I longed to be able to carry my share of the burden of making a living so we could stay together. I was only a boy of eight, and there was nothing substantial I could do as yet. The thing that kept me going each day and from crying each night was her promise to come get me as soon as possible. Each day when we went out to play, I looked for her, and each evening I waited, expecting to hear her voice at any time.

True to her word, Mom had been back to visit me the next Sunday. I couldn't help being unhappy when she left, and I held on to her skirt and begged to go with her.

"Please, I can take care of myself. I won't go in the streets, and I'll fix the meals and have them ready when you come home from work."

"We've been through this before, Son. Eight is too young to be alone in an apartment; all kinds of bad things could happen. You wouldn't want me to worry while at work, would you?"

It was so; I didn't want her to worry. She had enough to do without worrying about me. The following week, she didn't come until visiting time was almost over. One of my uncles brought her. She explained they had been looking for a place to live where I could join her, and there would be someone to take care of me. When I complained about her coming so late, she replied sharply, "After all, Sunday is my only day off." She looked so young and especially pretty, even though she was angry with me. I longed to climb into her lap and stay there forever. Her tone had hurt me, and so I said very little. It was a long time before I fell asleep that night.

The visits became farther and farther apart. Some Sundays, she didn't come at all. I always waited at the fence, hoping each person that passed by would be her. Sometimes someone in the distance would look like her, and my heart would beat loud inside me, but as they drew closer, I would see my mistake, and my disappointment engulfed me, drowning me in my lonesomeness and longing.

Then she stopped coming at all. I existed from Sunday to Sunday, always believing she would appear. Lately, I refused to participate in any outdoor games with the other children. I wanted to see her the minute she arrived, and besides, if she saw me preoccupied, she might leave without seeing me.

Up until my father died, there had been no uncles, but suddenly they began to appear every week, and mother seemed to be happier when they were around. I didn't understand this, for I felt the two of us should be enough. Now I pushed on, determined to find out why she hadn't come to get me the way she had promised. "Oh, Mother," I said over and over to myself, "please be home."

I must have walked for a couple of hours before I saw the familiar park we often visited on Sundays. The man who sold hot dogs was there in his usual place, but I had no money. My loneliness lessened as I passed by the small zoo in the park and saw some of the animals we had seen many times before. Mom and I had loved this park with its big green trees and beautiful flowers. It was like an oasis for us in the concrete jungle of the streets. I still had a long walk before I found Bowker Street, so I didn't stop but only glanced at the people feeding the pigeons as I passed by. It was past midafternoon, and the shadows had begun to lengthen. Pulling my sweater closer, I began to walk faster.

My legs were tired, and my body trembled with fatigue when I finally reached the old neighborhood where we had lived together so happily. I ran towards the cleaning shop and up the backstairs where I had waited for my mother every evening. The door was locked, so I knocked and waited.

A strange, funny-looking woman cracked open the door, put out her head covered with green curlers, and started screaming that she didn't want anyone to bother her. I asked for my mother, and she said no one lived there but she and her husband. They had moved in three months before, and she had never heard of my mother. I felt sick with disappointment at not finding her there and terribly distraught at my predicament. It was dusk, and the cleaning shop was closed, so I couldn't ask them where she was. The streets were deserted, and I was cold, alone, frightened, and hungry. There was nothing left to do but start back towards the foster home.

The streetlights came on. Except for an occasional passerby and the sound of the distant street cars, I was by myself. I kept wondering where my mother had moved. Probably she found a larger place and was getting it all fixed up for us and would come after me when it was ready.

I found the night had turned the once-friendly park into a menacing, frightening place. The wind through the trees and the roar of the loons all sounded different in the dark. I was overwhelmed with my plight and felt disaster was about to descend upon me at every turn. Looking over my shoulder, running as fast as I could, I bumped head-on into a young couple strolling arm-in-arm through the park. They asked what I was doing on the street so late, and I told them I was lost and was looking for the foster home. They walked me to the streetcar, gave me a nickel for carfare, and sent me on my way.

The people at the "home" seemed relieved to have me

come back. I guess they were worried; at least they said so. I got a severe tongue-lashing and had my privileges taken away for one month. No more desserts, playing in the yard or going to the library. They must have known that reading was my favorite pastime.

Later in bed, when it was all over, I cried for my mother. But I wasn't alone. I know that somewhere in that city, she was crying for me, too. I fell asleep and dreamed that tomorrow would be the day she would come and take me away with her forever.

The Girl Who Looked Like Elizabeth Taylor

"D'-d'-damn you Lila, l'-l'-listen to me. I said I'm l'-leaving you. I'm getting a d'-divorce!"

Lila, reposing on a chaise, moved the hand mirror up closer to her face. Relief flooded over her when she saw what she had thought was a new line was only a shadow. There had been a time when the words crow's feet had meant just what they said, but no longer, and lately, she had become more concerned about those beginning to appear around her eyes.

Up until she heard the word divorce, Lila had been paying no attention whatsoever to Roger. He had been raving and ranting at her for the past half hour. Now for the first time, she began to listen. Glancing up from the mirror, she favored him with her sweet smile, usually reserved for special people she wanted to charm.

Her voice matched her smile when she asked, "Roger, what do you think I should wear to the club dance this Friday? Do I look better in the red lace or the black velvet gown?"

"You think I'm not serious, that I'm not going through with the divorce."

She continued, "Linda Albert has a new Dior, but frankly, it doesn't matter what she wears; it always looks like a rag on her."

"I'm seeing an attorney tomorrow," he interrupted, "I already have an appointment. I bet you'll believe me when he calls you."

"If you'll come home early Friday, we can make it to the cocktail party the Browns are having. If you can't make it, I'll go with the Alberts, and you can meet me at the club later." Lila was now filing her nails carefully, meticulously, and completely absorbed in what she was doing.

His face livid with rage, he shouted, "I can take your absolute disregard of me. I never expected any more from you, but I can't sit by and watch you completely neglect the two boys. Half the time, they don't know who their mother is–it's a tossup between the cook and the maid. They're being brought up like two d'-d'-dogs. Your only concern is your damn everlasting self."

Funny, comical man, she thought. Short, fat, and almost bald, who could ever take him seriously? He looked like Humpty Dumpty, and certainly, he was acting as if he were cracked. How funny, she must remember that one to tell at the bridge club. It ought to be good for a couple of laughs at least. Lila knew her friends often speculated about her reason for marrying someone so ludicrous in appearance and speech.

There had been many handsome men that had wanted to marry her. She knew that she could never be happy with someone that matched or surpassed her appearance.

When she was with Roger, there was such a contrast that

her beauty became two-fold. There certainly was no competition there. She leaned forward now to catch a glimpse of herself in the wall mirror.

Her mother and friends had been telling her for years how she resembled Elizabeth Taylor. Convinced of this, she had her beautician style her hair in the latest Elizabeth Taylor fashion. She wore the same type of clothes, delighting in the ones with extreme cleavage. When Roger protested she was revealing too much of herself, she gave him a disdainful look, and he said no more. A pair of violet contact lenses took care of eyes that were regretfully brown. Lila often wondered what the famous actress's reaction would be if she accidentally ran into her on the street. This musing made for much daydreaming.

Keeping up her looks became more difficult each year. It meant more days and longer hours spent at the beauty shop, and makeup had become a chore. Whatever effort she expended was made well with her by the sensation her appearance always created.

Roger's voice broke into her thoughts again. "You and your crazy preoccupation with Elizabeth Taylor—I'm fed up; it's too much."

He went into the bedroom, and she could hear the opening and closing of drawers. He was just bluffing. Bored and tired of his stupidity, having lost all patience, she shouted to him, "You wouldn't dare leave me. I'll have the boys. Everyone knows judges favor the mother. Furthermore, there isn't another woman living who would look at you. Humpty Dumpty, Humpty Dumpty," she ridiculed in a high falsetto.

He came out of the bedroom, suitcase in hand. "I'm going to a hotel. You'll hear from my lawyer tomorrow."

Wait until she told Sybil about this; it was positively a riot. Without looking up from the magazine she was reading, she said, "Oh, go unpack your things. You're not going anywhere, little man. You've had your fun and been the big man for all of …" she paused and looked at the diamond watch he had given her for their first anniversary, "Thirty-five minutes."

"Damn you, damn you, damn you," he said between clenched teeth.

She raised her head and noticed for the first time the gun partially hidden by the overcoat thrown over his arm. Before she could protest, he fired five times. She slumped back over the chaise, face towards the ceiling, still posing even in death.

The police found him kneeling beside her body, crying, holding her limp hand in his. When the coroner ordered her body put on the stretcher, Roger took one last long look before the blanket was drawn over her face.

"She does look like Elizabeth Taylor, doesn't she?" he asked one of the attendants.

"Yeah," one of them replied, "She does a little bit at that."

Duty

Maude Meriwether was quite aware of the picture she made sitting patiently outside the United States Immigration Office—tiny, gray-haired, sweet-faced, dressed in a very chic orchid knit suit. She resembled a typical modern-day grandmother. The serene picture she made was far from what she actually felt, for inside Mrs. Meriwether was quite perturbed.

"Why shouldn't I be?" she thought. "This is a terrible position I've been forced into, destroying another human being's chance for happiness."

Thirty minutes later, she was ushered into the office of the immigration official, Lester T. Brown. Infuriated at being kept waiting, she kept her anger hidden—showing her distaste by looking at her watch several times, sighing, and smiling politely. She noticed that Mr. Brown got the message, for he apologized profusely for keeping her waiting.

Maude was seated in the chair beside Lester T. Brown's desk. After the usual social amenities, the weather and such, she waited for the usual, "And what can we do for you, Mrs. Meriwether?"

"I hesitated to come here. Really, I did. But I knew that it would be unpatriotic if I stayed away and withheld vital information from you. I consider it my duty as a good cit-

izen to come forward with this story." She had been leaning forward in the chair while addressing Mr. Brown, but
now she leaned back and made herself comfortable before
continuing.

"Two years ago, my gardener, who is of Mexican de-
scent, brought a young woman from Mexico to live with
me. This was at my request since I'm widowed and live
alone. The girl was named Juana Morales and spoke not
one word of English. All the possessions she had in the
world were in the paper sack she carried. I really never
should have taken her because she had a husband and a
tiny baby in Mexico, but she was so pathetic and needed
the work so badly I just couldn't turn her down.

"My gardener explained that the husband had a job, but
the wages are so low in Mexico that what he made wasn't
enough to feed the three of them, and there was no work
for her at all in the town she came from. She only comes
here to make money to send back. She was happy to get
any salary I gave her. I must say on her behalf she was the
hardest worker I've ever seen. However, since she was un-
trained, I paid her just a little more than half what my
friends paid their negro maids. This was more money than
she could have ever dreamed of making in Mexico.

"You've never seen such a maid; my friends were green
with envy. She never once took a day off. That isn't as
strange as it sounds. After all, where did she have to go?
Systematically, she washed every window in the house, and
when she finished the last one, she would start over again.
I must admit, she learned fast because soon she was not

only washing my car but doing all my sewing.

"The truth of the matter is that since there were just the two of us, there just wasn't enough work for her to do. You've heard the old maxim, 'the devil finds work for idle hands.' I surely didn't want that to happen, so I let my daughter-in-law have her every Thursday. On Fridays, she always helped my invalid friend down the street, and on Saturdays, the people next door. Juana cleaned their house from top to bottom. If my daughter-in-law ever gave me a hard time about anything, I just didn't send Juana over.

"None of them paid her. You know I couldn't accept money from my invalid friend, although she offered it. I considered my son's house part of the family, and the people next door are always doing me favors; it was the least I could do for them. She was getting paid more than she ever had before, plus the privilege of living in a decent house with good food. Do you realize, Mr. Brown, that in the town she came from, there was no running water?"

Lester T. Brown spoke again, "Just what is it about Mrs. Morales I should know, Mrs. Meriwether?"

Maude Meriwether looked down at her spotless white gloves resting on the orchid-knit skirt and continued, "Six months ago, against my better judgment, Juana went home for her child's second birthday. When she returned, she told me she must leave me; she could no longer live away from her family. I certainly am not going to be responsible for separating a family. It just isn't right for a husband and wife to live apart like that. So, I made the ultimate sacrifice; I put my good name on the dotted line with the federal government and brought the husband, Manuel, and little girl to the United States legally. I don't know anyone else that would have done as much for this girl. It was for my effort that Juana smiled and sang all the time.

"It was very difficult the day the husband and baby arrived. They spoke no English, and besides, I'm used to my privacy, and having a man around was an annoyance. I told Juana to tell him they could stay there with me for a couple of days, but after that, they must find a place for themselves. I suggested they put the baby in a nursery with some good Spanish woman. The husband could get a room somewhere, and Juana could see him occasionally. When I signed for this man to come into the States, I promised the government I would be personally responsible for them. That the only work he would do was in the household. That's the law, as you know."

"Did he have work in a household, Mrs. Meriwether?" Mr. Brown inquired.

"When I signed for the husband and the child, I had to guarantee that between Juana and her husband, the two would make $300 a month–another law I might remind you, Mr. Brown. Now, I certainly can't afford that kind of money. I have five or six charities I give to already. So, I took my valuable time to call my loyal friends and line up jobs for him. I had no trouble doing this. All my friends were quite willing to help him out. I promised them that he would do all their woodwork, walls, and windows for $5 a day. Do you realize a white man or a negro would charge at least $15 a day for the same amount of work? If he worked each day, plus the salary I gave her, they would easily make $300 a month, and I was within the law. One thing I've always been Mr. Brown is a law-abiding citizen. The late Mr. Meriwether, may God rest his soul, used to say I was the most law-abiding person he knew."

"You certainly are a very conscientious person, Mrs. Meriwether. The world would most certainly be a better place if there were more people like you."

"Thank you, Mr. Brown, but sometimes people who try to do the right thing for others are often sorely disappointed. I didn't lift a hand to help them. I figured that it was best to let them stand on their own two feet. The gardener didn't offer to help them, and I felt if their own people wouldn't help, why should I do any more than my share? Surely, I had done enough already. Juana's husband knew a Mexican couple who lived on the other side of the city. The husband took the little girl and rode the bus over to their house and rented a room from them.

"Don't you know that must have been funny? Neither the father nor the baby knew a word of English. Can't you just see what a scream it must have been trying to explain to the bus drivers just where they wanted to go? I just wish I could have been a mouse and followed them. I understand it took them almost a day to get there. You know, these Mexicans are used to riding buses. Hardly anyone in the small Mexican towns can afford a car. I'm sure you've seen pictures of them with their pigs and chickens on the buses in Mexico. They just don't know any better. You certainly wouldn't ever catch me on a bus with a pig.

"I thought all's well that ends well, but I spoke too soon. About two weeks later I woke up and found the husband and the baby were back. In my house! Can you imagine the nerve? Taking advantage of my hospitality! I was so mad, I refused to leave my bedroom. Juana brought my breakfast in. She always brought my breakfast to bed, and I told her plenty. They had better be out by noon. She cried and told me the night before the Mexican couple they were staying with had a big fight. I guess you know how hot-headed the Mexicans can be. In her anger, the woman had locked not only her own husband out of the house, but Juana's husband and baby too. Something about being tired of all the extra work. Now wouldn't you think after two weeks he would have something else lined up?

"The next stunt she pulled didn't catch me by surprise. I knew the next thing she'd want was Saturday and Sunday off to go see them. She was sadly mistaken if she thought I was going to have my routine interfered with just because she had a couple of relations down the road. When Juana asked, as I knew she would, I told her that from now on part of her job was to baby sit with my two grandchildren every Saturday night. She had her head down, looking humble. That's another thing: these Mexicans and their humility. It's all a pose just to get to you. You do understand don't you, Mr. Brown? Give these people an inch, and they'll end up taking a mile.

"She didn't protest, but early Sunday morning before I was up, she left the house, walked a mile to the city bus lines, rode it eighteen miles to the center of town, then caught another bus for the forty-five-mile ride to where he was. If he was any kind of a man, he would have come in to see her. I had no objections to him visiting her in my home Sunday afternoons. She didn't return until Monday, and I was fit to be tied. You see, Mondays I do volunteer work at the hospital. I had to call them and say I couldn't come—the first time I've missed in years. It was all I could do to control myself, but I didn't reprimand her. I just didn't speak to her the rest of the week.

"For the record, I want to make it clear: I believe Juana was a good person and would be if it weren't for her husband's influence. He called her several times a week. Once he told her the baby was sick. Have you ever heard such nonsense? The child didn't have a sick day in that filthy country she came from, but he expected me to believe she was sick here in the country where everything is nice and clean.

"Every Sunday morning from then on Juana would go join her husband and return at noon Monday. Mr. Brown, I want the federal government to clearly understand that I warned them what would happen if they did not both work as domestics in a household. He had a job working in the field, and if he ever got caught there would be trouble with the authorities. I had all these jobs lined up for him. My friends were quite willing to hire him, but no, poor ignorant people, he couldn't understand when someone was trying to help them.

"Once when he called, I refused to let Juana talk with him. I told her, 'Your husband acts like a baby. He has no right to call and bother you when you are working. He should start acting like a grown man and resume adult responsibilities.' She didn't answer me because she knew I was right. For two years, this girl had been with me and had not been ill one day. She began having headaches. Sometimes they were so bad she was blinded temporarily. I paid no attention because I knew they were caused by nerves. She would never have had a headache if it hadn't been for that thoughtless beast of a husband worrying her.

"Now, this is why I'm here: one month ago, Juana left as usual on Sunday. After she had gone, I noticed not all, but most of her clothes were gone. These clothes weren't hers to take. My friends had given them to her. Things of theirs they no longer wanted. She certainly did all right for herself, coming to me with a paper sack and leaving with a closet full of clothes, and let me assure you, my friends buy only the best.

"I've heard from her just once since then. She called to say a doctor had told her she needed a rest. Only a fool that didn't know better would believe that, and I'm no fool."

Mr. Brown leaned forward and asked, "Now just exactly what is it you're here for Mrs. Meriwether?"

"I want to make it very clear Mr. Brown, that I want to rescind sponsoring this man and child in this country. They are breaking the law every day they are here. Perfectly good American men could use the job he has. There is no point in taking food from the mouths of our own good citizens. I no longer want to be responsible for someone who is obviously committing a crime."

"And Juana," he asked, "what about her?"

"I might consider taking her back. I'm not certain. I had always thought of her as being completely honest, but Mr. Brown, I really don't want to mention it but since you brought it up, I'm missing three glove stretchers. There was no one else in that house but the two of us. You know, all this has ruined my faith in human nature."

"Mrs. Meriwether, you've done a great service by coming here today, and I assure you the United States Immigration Department will see that justice is done."

Mr. Brown stood up to indicate the interview was over, "Thank you again for coming." He helped the dainty, little lady to her feet.

"I hope I haven't given you the impression I don't like immigrants. My grandparents were immigrants. They came from Europe." A trace of tears filled her eyes. "It broke my heart to think how much easier it would have been for them if only someone had put out a helping hand for them, as I did for these ungrateful people."

She straightened her collar in a little helpless gesture, and suddenly took his hand in her pure, white-gloved ones, "Why God bless you Mr. Brown for the good work you're doing."

After the door closed behind her, Mr. Brown thumbed through the telephone book until he found what he was looking for, and then dialed a number.

"This is Lester T. Brown from the U.S. Immigration Office. I have a Mexican couple and child who need to work in a household for one year and receive at least $300 a month."

He listened to the other party and then said, "Wonderful. A job on a ranch is perfect. Thank you. Send me the details and I'll personally bring them over."

He then rang the buzzer for his secretary. "Miss Jones, take a letter. It's to Juana and Manuel Morales. Let it begin, 'My Dearest Friends, as your new sponsor let me welcome you to the United States ...'"

Honest John

John Upton earned the nickname "Honest John" very early in life, for he was known by his friends, family, and teachers to be completely on the up and up no matter what the situation. He never pushed ahead in line, taking "a cut" as the other children called it.

If his teacher reprimanded him for not knowing his lesson well, he never alibied, but readily admitted, "I didn't study well enough." This was the same at home, a little annoying at times to the adults because it kept their consciences working overtime.

John progressed not in an outstanding fashion but steadily and slowly, first through high school, a six-month business course, and into a job as a clerk at a branch bank. From there, not because of any brilliance but because of his constant honesty and dependability, he was promoted to a larger bank and to the position of head cashier.

Honest John Upton met and married a bank employee. He soon found himself in the world of time payments, home loans, insurance payments, and so on.

His wife became bored with his everlasting honesty, but the bank found his honesty to their liking, and soon Honest John found himself vice-president, assistant to another vice-president. John was quite satisfied with himself, but his wife's boredom bothered him not at all because at least she was honest about it and made no attempt to hide it from him.

Then into his Garden of Eden crept a snake by the name of Eric Masters, his seldom seen brother-in-law, who not being honest, had become involved with a gambling syndicate. Having lost money to them and unable to pay he was being forced with extinction, his own.

In desperation, he turned to his newly acquired brother for help. He begged Honest John to supply the much-needed money, but John, who was up to his neck in debt, declined.

Eric pleaded with him to "borrow from the bank" but John was horrified at the thought of such a dishonest action. The pleading, and crying, both from Eric and his wife, finally moved John and he agreed to "borrow" the money temporarily and repay it later with money Eric promised was available.

This was the first dishonest act John had ever perpetrated. After it was done, and so skillfully that not a trace of the deed was to be found, John was wracked with tremendous waves of guilt. When asleep he suffered nightmares and would wake up bathed in sweat.

Several weeks later he was called into the bank president's office and told they were so proud of his honesty that they felt it should be rewarded. A banquet was to be held, the most important people in the city to be invited, and John was to be honored.

It was then John broke down, confessed all, and the bank president left him to dash into the inner workings of the bank and check the books. He checked, the bank examiner checked, everyone in the bank checked, but nowhere was there a shortage to be found. They all agreed then that Honest John Upton was overworked and was simply having a hallucination of sorts.

Honest John returned to work; the banquet postponed. He lasted three days when he broke down hysterically at work. Nothing could quiet him; the doctor was called, and John was sent to a sanitarium.

There he remains. A very ordinary guy. The only thing the nurses say in their reports to the doctor that comes out once a month to see him is that Honest John is a habitual liar, never telling the truth about anything.

The Avenging Angel

A familiar sight, Mom Adams walked slowly down the street. Today she was preoccupied and had no time to gossip. Afraid she might be stopped by one of the friendly storekeepers, she kept her head down, glancing up only when forced to at a busy intersection. Occasionally, she leaned on her cane and felt in her paper shopping bag to make certain her newspaper was still there. Her reason for hurrying was a story it contained about a murder and suicide, both for which she was responsible.

She wore the same black coat winter and summer, pulled close around her as protection against the elements. Except for her pure white hair pulled up by a hairnet, she appeared to be what she was—a little old lady dressed in black.

The entire neighborhood knew her well, for she walked these same sidewalks daily. They thought of her as a dear, sweet soul. This was her real protection, not her coat. Her sweet smile, known to every waitress, clerk, and bus driver, was a well-practiced facade that hid hate whose depths were unknown even to herself.

She hurried on, anxious for the privacy of her apartment where in her own good time she could read and savor the story in the paper. Her latest accomplishment was a supreme feat, and she shivered with anticipation.

Mom Adams hadn't always been this way. Once she was a happily married woman, and her smile meant what it said. Until one day, her husband ran off with his secretary. At first, she was hurt and bewildered, going through the motions of making a new life for herself. In later years she became lonely, bitter, and hateful. It was by accident that she had stumbled into her new role, that of avenger.

She had been resting in the lobby of a hotel when she had overheard a conversation between two people planning a tryst and not with their own spouses. Inflamed, projecting herself into the place of the wronged wife, she knew what she must do. It wasn't easy, but her duty was clear.

By inquiries of the bell boys and the hotel clerk, she found out the names of the two, for who would suspect such a dear little old lady of ulterior motives? A phone call to the woman's husband did the rest. The pleasure she received after reading in the paper that the husband had almost beaten his wife to death for her infidelity was compensation enough. It spurred her on to seek out and find people who were sinful and see that they were punished.

It was a large city, and she circulated everywhere. Early each morning found her on the street, her plans laid out for the day. Flushing out these people wasn't easy, but she managed by perseverance to track them down. It meant hours and sometimes days of sitting in railway terminals, bus stations, and back booths in out-of-the-way restaurants. When the going was slow, she enlarged her territory to cover prostitutes and drug pushers. She would call the police from the nearest phone booth if she were the least bit suspicious. Occasionally, she would read about a false arrest, but she triumphed when she caused a ring of call girls to be broken up.

The newspapers mentioned her only as an anonymous tipster, but she liked to think of herself as The Avenging Angel. The title came from a television show she had seen and admired.

Once more, she patted the newspaper—petted it would be more accurate, for this particular exposé had been a real coup. She had every reason to be proud. When she called the husband at his office, he had been disbelieving and called her vile names. This didn't stop her but only spurred her further with more accusations. By the time she hung up, he was convinced.

The wife was a different story. She had been indignant, denying everything. This was a new twist, usually she begged for mercy.

At last Mom Adams was in her apartment seated in the kitchen, the newspaper spread before her. There were three pictures in the paper: the husband, the wife, and the wife's brother. It was with shock and disbelief she recognized the brother as the man she had thought was the lover. The headlines read, "Anonymous Call Causes Tragedy."

For two days and sleepless nights, she wrestled with her conscience. Her despair was genuine, but then it suddenly occurred to her that some higher power was testing her, seeing if she could take success as well as failure. It was the devil who had sent the bother to fool her. With horror she realized she almost hadn't passed the test.

On the third day, she again donned her black coat, took her cane from behind the door, and once more went out into the wicked city. The Avenging Angel had work to do. She had been given a sign, and it was her duty to purge the world of sin.

As she passed her neighbors on the street, she nodded her head and smiled. It was not surprising to overhear someone say to her, "Don't stay away so long Mom, we miss your sweet smile. It just isn't the same around here without you."

The Mayor

Edna and Earl Yeager were being forced to face reality and make drastic changes in their way of life. Thirty years of living beyond their means had finally caught up with them.

They had been young and ambitious when they made their first down payment on a house in the highest-priced neighborhood the city had to offer. Their rationale had been that by starting big and looking the part, Earl would go further in his new job as head cashier at the bank. The money for this auspicious beginning came from the finance company, but this debt was of no real concern because they both knew it was but a matter of time until Earl was promoted to a higher position with more salary.

Living in an exclusive neighborhood brought on other financial obligations that they had not anticipated. That is, keeping up with the Joneses or not being accepted socially. It took a lot of doing to dress the part, pay for a gardener, buy a new car each year, and entertain in the manner that was expected. Often, they found themselves in the ludicrous position of wearing expensive clothes, seated at their expensive dining table eating peanut butter sandwiches, which was all they could afford.

The worst part was the trips. It was imperative that they travel if they were to remain with the "in" group. Several times when their annual two weeks' vacation came around, and they had no money for extras; they spent the entire time in an inexpensive local hotel reading books on Hawaii and sitting under a sunlamp. When they returned, they were welcomed back and became known among their crowd as real aficionados of the islands. It wasn't unusual to hear, "Ask Earl or Edna about the service at the Royal Hawaiian Hotel. If anyone knows, they do. Why, they practically lived there last year."

Although Earl was a conscientious worker, the promotion at the bank didn't come as anticipated. After seven years, he was made one of the many second-vice presidents, which gave him more status, but little extra money. To their dismay and disappointment, younger men bypassed him, plus there were others at the bank that had seniority and couldn't be bypassed. At the end of thirty years, he was retired and given a gold watch. The pension and his social security gave him two hundred dollars a month for life. This was all they had besides the equity in their house, which came to eleven thousand dollars. It just wasn't enough for him to continue living in the same neighborhood. So, they sold their house, took the equity, and moved to a small town to avoid the embarrassment of accidentally running into friends.

The town Earl selected had a population of five thousand, was on a secondary state road, and a good one hundred miles from the city they came from. Edna, too disturbed and upset at giving up her home and friends, had not been much help in moving.

Earl rented the finest apartment available for fifty-five

dollars a month. Where they had lived, a garage for their car would have cost more. The next morning after they were settled, Earl went to the town's only bank and deposited the eleven-thousand-dollar equity check. The clerk asked if he wanted the money put in a savings account. Earl casually waved his hand and told them to put it in checking.

What Earl and Edna didn't know was that small-town banks are unlike big-city banks in that they keep very little secret. Before the day was out, the entire town was agog with the talk of the new affluent residents.

The next day the bank president's wife called on Edna and invited her to join her study club and to come for dinner. Soon after, a delegation of three from the local Rotary Club came to welcome Earl and ask him to join their group. It wasn't many more days that they had more invitations than they could handle. Their life became full of more daily activity than they had ever known in the city.

With their fine clothes and acquired sophisticated big-city manners, they rose quickly to a position of importance. Earl bought a thousand dollars of stock in the bank and was promptly asked to become a member of the board of directors. This gave him an enviable position because now he was in on all the important business transactions going on in the area.

Without consulting Edna, Earl made several small investments that came his way and managed to double and triple his money. He now really understood the adage "the rich get richer" because that was what he continued to do

... get richer. He kept all this from Edna, intending to surprise her on their wedding anniversary.

Edna was not doing too badly herself. Accustomed to years of penny-pinching to "keep up" appearances and maintain her status, she was managing beautifully on the two hundred dollars a month. The demands now just weren't as much. Where Champagne had once been important, beer would do just as well.

The day of their anniversary was one Earl had been looking forward to. He couldn't wait to see the surprise on Edna's face when he told her they wouldn't have to worry about money anymore. His plan was to give her the bank book filled with all those figures and watch her amazement at what he had accomplished.

But first, in a teasing fashion, he asked, "Edna, if you had all the money we ever dreamed of having, what would be the first thing you would do?"

She replied, "I'd move out of this hick town so fast your head would spin."

"But I thought you liked my being a director at the bank and a member of the Rotary? Why even today, some of the fellows were talking about putting me up for city council!"

"What good is the city council when you're living around people that don't know a veal parmesan from a chocolate souffle, or a Dior from a Givenchy."

Earl was stunned. This last he hadn't expected. "Put your coat on, dear; I'm taking you out to dinner tonight at the Blue Moon Cafe. We're going to celebrate thirty-one years together."

Janice Ruth Anchell

He patted the breast coat of his pocket and felt the bank book still there, unopened. He supposed he would have to forgo the pleasure of seeing her face when she found out about the money, but he had an idea that she would like being a wealthy widow. Not that he was planning on dying anytime soon. No sir. After a few years on the city council, he sure wouldn't mind being mayor for a while.

Of Mice and Mothers

The best-laid plans of mice and mothers often go astray, as I so well know. My husband and I had great plans for the weekend, but they have to be canceled. We can't very well go anywhere since Stephen, our thirteen-year-old is going on a hardship campout and needs our help.

This campout is to be so rugged that even the scoutmaster isn't going.

"Part of the hardship," Stephen explained.

The boys plan to spend the weekend high in the mountain snow, sleeping in tents. Everything they're taking, cooking equipment, food, clothes, etc., has to be carried the last three miles.

This is the one time my middle name should have been "organized" for I had bought waterproofing spray and waterproofed everything he was taking. I didn't know there was such a thing as waterproofing spray, and neither did the ten stores we went to before we finally found it.

An extra heavy warm coat had to be purchased. The one he owns wasn't heavy enough, and no one we knew had an old one he could borrow. He had even tried on his father's size forty, which was great, except his hands were so far up the sleeves they would have been useless, and it hung on his frame like a folded tent.

I avoided this last purchase right up until the last minute;

for how long can you wear a heavy coat in Southern California? And how long will it fit a growing thirteen-year-old?

His lunch was packed, for on the first day they didn't plan to cook until evening. This I put together with great pleasure despite his protest of "Please, Mom, no one ever brings as much lunch as I do. It's embarrassing."

As each item went into the sack, I visualized him as he discovered each carefully selected morsel. How his eyes would widen when he saw not one, but two, pastrami sandwiches on a kaiser roll. He would nod appreciatively when he saw the Washington Delicious apple. It had to be from Washington; he says there is a difference. Would he like the new kind of potato chip? I doubted it since he made a face when I told him they were onion flavored, but surely, I'd be redeemed when he found the cherry pie, the bubble gum, and the candy bar.

No running around at the last minute for me, everything had been carefully and deliberately assembled, and now I was free to make plans of my own with my husband and the other four children.

I was free until his Patrol Leader called and said he was in bed with the flu. Do you know what an A.P.L. is? Neither did I. It stands for Assistant Patrol Leader, and that's what Stephen happens to be. That meant he had to buy all the food for his patrol for the entire weekend. Also, all the cooking equipment had to be washed and packed.

It doesn't sound very difficult, but we only had one evening to do it, and at ten o'clock at night we were still in the kitchen washing potatoes and celery. Our last job was wrapping a dozen eggs separately so that they wouldn't break.

He left this morning at 6:00 A.M. I know; I had to get up to drive him to the rendezvous, but he had coffee made for me, and he looked so excited and happy. You have to be very young to be excited and happy about sleeping three days in the snow.

We only had to turn back once, and that was to get his gloves.

Happy hardship camp, Steve. As for me, I'm going back to bed. I'm already tired, and I haven't even been anywhere.

Point of Attack

Sam Feinberg looked out the front window of his small delicatessen and saw the street was quite empty except for a few children playing ball in the fading twilight. He decided to wait five minutes, and if the young man didn't come by, then he would close and go home. Mixed feelings of relief flooded over him because he had been dreading the coming encounter, but now he would have another at home, which might be worse.

Last night he had promised his wife, Molly, he'd bring the young man home to meet their daughter, Frieda. Molly always came home from weddings upset, but the one yesterday had been the worst yet. Her sister's youngest daughter, barely nineteen, had been married to a young intern. Their own daughter would be thirty on her next birthday without a prospect in sight. They had already done everything possible to see she met eligible men but to no avail.

Molly's tears had driven him frantic. In desperation, he told her of a young man who had been coming into the store several times a week, who had just moved to the city and knew no one. At this news, Mollie straightened up and ceased her crying to ask questions about him. He made up answers, probably truths, but he was still guessing. The boy was a student (of what he didn't know), obviously poor, but very smart, tall, thin …

"Poor boy, we'll have to feed him," she interrupted. He wore glasses, was friendly, but a trifle shy.

"Sam," Molly had asked, "Will you bring him home?"

"Certainly."

"When?"

"So how do I know? Don't pin me down."

"When?" she asked again.

"Tomorrow, maybe. He always comes in on Saturday nights."

"What for?"

"For food, Molly. For heaven's sake, what do you think I sell there? Enough of the third degree."

"I'll tell Frieda." She started to leave the room.

"No, Molly, not this time. Let it be casual like I knew before."

They had left it at that and gone to bed, but this morning as he left for work, Molly had reminded him of his promise. All evening he had been waiting for the nameless man. It probably was a waste of time; he would be just like the other young men, customers of his he had brought home. Most of them accepted, anxious for a good meal and an evening in a real home. Their eagerness turned to dismay when they realized the reason for the invitation. One look at his beloved Frieda, an evening in her spiritless presence, and they would disappear, never to be seen again.

He and Molly adored their only child and had watched over her like lions and their cub since she was born. Perhaps too much, he sighed.

A husband had to be fond of her, especially if he and

Molly were to enjoy any grandchildren. The urgency was there, or he wouldn't be resorting to such last-ditch measures as inviting strangers into his home, much less sitting in his empty store thirty minutes after closing time.

The five minutes were up. Sam drew the blinds and began to lock the door, but a sudden rapping on the front glass of the store made him jump back.

A male voice called, "Mr. Feinberg, Mr. Feinberg, am I too late?"

Sam looked out the window and saw it was the young man standing in the cold, his collar turned up over his ears.

"No, my boy, come in," and he began unlocking the door. "You're just in time."

This one, he thought to himself, won't get away.

The Peach

Awakened in the early morning hours by threatening thunder, I jumped from the bed and ran to the window. A storm had just begun, and immediately my first thought was for my peach.

I had been watching the peach tree for two months now. Each day as I walked past it on my way to the clothesline, I would stop to examine the branch that came over into my yard. Last year my neighbor, who owned the tree, said all the peaches on my side of the fence belonged to me, and since it was a lone branch that hung over, I coveted it like a miser with her gold.

Those same peaches could have been purchased at any grocery store or roadside stand, but it wouldn't have been the same. My delight in this one lone branch was the nostalgia and memories it brought back of childhood, climbing into the top branches of a tree, bracing myself with my feet against one of the limbs, sinking my teeth into the delicious, firm meat of the peach. Best of all, in a tree, there was no limit—you could eat to your heart's content.

I first realized it was spring when I saw my branch covered with tiny, delicate pink blossoms. The bees had seen them, too, and hovered above, taking their nectar and making a promise of things to come. I examined the blossoms with a practiced eye, estimating how many would, in time, perform a miracle and become fruit.

After the blossoms disappeared, tiny green nubs, no bigger than the head of a small nail, took their place. Long, slim green leaves appeared, and the miracle was ready to begin. These same nubs were to become the peaches I was looking for. My pleasure grew each day with the swell of the nubs, and the daily baskets of clothes I carried felt lighter as I eagerly stopped by my branch to see how it was doing.

Now grown large and round but still hard and green, I selected one with a faint blush. I decided it was to be called "The Chosen One." This was the one I would eat secretly, quietly, all by myself. The others I would bring in and share with my family. It was only this first peach that had significance for me now.

How fast The Chosen One grew, far outstripping the others in its growth. How wise I had been to select it. My secret I kept to myself. To others, peaches suddenly appeared one day, but to me, it had become a very personal matter.

Now the storm threatened overhead, and I, foolish person with so much to do, worried about a peach. I knew the wind would soon dash it to the ground because only the day before, I had noticed the limb was bent, burdened with heavy fruit. I could have had my peach then but had decided to wait just one more day. I ran into the yard, the wind whipping my hair and robe around me. The Chosen One was still hanging tenaciously to its stem. I pulled it and felt it release its hold. Perfect, as I knew it would be, I returned to the house, holding the peach and feeling its soft, light fuzz on my hand.

It sat on my kitchen cabinet, and occasionally I would give it a cursory glance while I busied myself fixing breakfast. It was as pretty as a picture, and I knew it would fulfill its promise.

Into the kitchen padded my sleepy five-year-old boy, James. My baby. The joy of my life, the one child not at school but home with me each day. His eyes widened when he saw the peach and he exclaimed, "What a funny-looking apple."

"That's not an apple; that's a peach."

"What's a peach?"

"Delicious fruit that grows on a tree. When I was a little girl, I had a peach tree in my yard."

"Mother, you were never a little girl; you're my mother." And then, "Mother, may I eat the peach?"

It's to my shame that I hesitated, but only for a moment.

"Of course, Jamie, you may have it."

The Chosen One was to be eaten by a wide-eyed cherub. Watching him bite, slowly, meticulously into each piece, my pleasure was doubled as he continued to savor my prize.

After he finished and the peach was reduced to a flesh-less pit, he flung it over his shoulder and said, "Thank you for the peach, Mother, but I like apples better."

I might have been disappointed had I eaten the peach and found it to be less than I had anticipated. If somehow its sweetness was lessened by the years gone by. How could

Janice Ruth Anchell

I expect my son to experience the feelings I had long ago high up in my childhood tree? There was no way. He would have to find his own tree.

Getting to Know Your Neighbors
by Bob Destino
The Costa Courier

"Madame President." That's a title Janice Anchell has had for much of her life. She was president of the PTA at her childrens' school in Houston, president of the 7,000-member Woman's Auxiliary of the Los Angeles County Medical Association, president of The Sisterhood of Beth Shalom Temple (Santa Monica), president of the Riviera Club of Orange County, and president of the Casta del Sol Republican Club which she co-founded and on whose Board of Directors she served for 30 years. She was also a board member of the Women's Division of the Los Angeles Chamber of Commerce. While living in the Los Angeles area, she co-founded the Pet Orphan's Fund, which now has its own building and veterinarian staff in the San Fernando Valley.

Janice was technically born in Canada, although her parents lived in Oklahoma. She became an official United States citizen when she was 26 years old. Her father was a medical doctor who cared for military personnel in the USA during World War II. The family moved so much during those years that Janice attended five different high schools. She attended Oklahoma University with a major in Journalism. While at OU, she was elected queen of two different campus clubs.

She and her late husband, Melvin, a nationally prominent M.D., had five children, seven grandchildren, and four great-grandchildren. Janice and Melvin were married for 61 years.